THROUGH
Love's
TRIALS

By
JULIE COULTER BELLON

spring creek
BOOK COMPANY
Provo, Utah

ISBN: 1-932898-14-X
e. 2
Published by:
Spring Creek Book Company
P.O. Box 50355
Provo, Utah 84605-0355
www. springcreekbooks.com
Cover design © Spring Creek Book Company
Printed in the United States of America
10 9 8 7 6 5 4 3 2 1
Printed on acid-free paper

Library of Congress Cataloging-in-Publication Data
Bellon, Julie Coulter, 1969-
 Through love's trials / by Julie Coulter Bellon.
 p. cm.
 ISBN 1-932898-14-X (pbk. : alk. paper)
 1. Attorney and client--Fiction. 2. Terrorism--Fiction. I. Title.
PS3602.E648T48 2004
813'.6--dc22

                        2004009584

DEDICATION

This book is dedicated to the love of my life, my husband Brian, who has always encouraged me to reach for my dreams.

ACKNOWLEDGMENTS

Thanks to my parents, Bob and Renee, for believing in me, and to the staff at Spring Creek Book Company for believing in the story. And last, but not least, I need to thank Jeffrey, Lauren, Jared, Jayden, Nathan and Brandon for their patience and understanding when Mom just needed to write one more thing. I love you!

PROLOGUE

Edward Carrington motioned to Paul James, the junior partner walking down the hall. "Would you please come into my office?"

"Uh, sure Mr. Carrington," Paul replied. He shifted the files under his arm and followed his boss into the office.

Waving Paul toward a seat, Edward sat down in his expensively upholstered leather chair behind a beautiful mahogany desk shined to perfection. "How long have you been at our firm now?" he asked.

"Just over a year, sir," Paul replied.

"Have you enjoyed working here?" Carrington asked.

"Yes, sir, the firm of Carrington, Stone and Wells was my first choice out of law school."

"We're glad you are here," Mr. Carrington stated. "You've done very well at carving a reputation for yourself as a defense attorney that we can count on." Carrington leveled his gaze. "Do you like to win, Paul?"

Paul smiled. "Yes, sir."

"What do you know about Vicente DiChesney?" he asked, watching Paul carefully from over the top of his glasses.

Paul swallowed. *Was this a test?* "Well, Mr. DiChesney is being charged with embezzlement and fraud, I believe. There are some rumors that he's tied to the mob."

"Do you believe those rumors?" Mr. Carrington asked.

Paul shifted the files on his lap, sensing this answer was very important. "Mr. Carrington, I'm a criminal defense attorney. My client's innocence or guilt will be determined by a jury of his peers and my job is to present the facts as my client instructs me—not to judge him."

Paul leaned back in his chair, meeting the senior partner's eyes head on. Those eyes glittered back at him from behind the small glasses. "Well done, son."

Edward pulled a file out from the top drawer of his desk, with a small white envelope on top. "I want you to take over the DiChesney file. I'll second chair you for this trial, but I'm looking forward to a long and happy arrangement with Vicente DiChesney and I think you are the man to help this firm achieve the . . . closeness we want with this client." He fingered the white envelope on top of the file. "It comes with a substantial raise and shot at being a full partner."

Paul took a deep breath as he opened the envelope. The six figure number made his eyes swim. "Yes, sir," was all he could manage to say.

Edward stood and Paul stood with him. "You'd best get started with the file. The preliminary hearing is in two days." Paul took the slim file and put it on top of the files he had brought in with him. "Give those other cases to another junior partner," he said, putting his arm around Paul. "You won't have time for them now with your new position."

Paul nodded and walked toward his own office, his mind racing. He couldn't wait to tell Emma. She would be so proud of him! He sat down at his desk and reached for the phone, then realized she wouldn't be home yet. He set down the files and singled out the DiChesney folder. He had to start prepping right away. It was their first wedding anniversary and they had plans for the evening. *I'll tell Emma my news then*, he thought happily. *She'll be so excited. We can buy all the things we've ever dreamed of.*

ℴℴ

Emma rubbed her abdomen, looking disbelievingly at the pregnancy test. It was a very bright blue. Shaking her head, a smile slowly spread across her face. A baby! Paul would be so surprised. She looked down at the little stick again, a frown replacing her smile. Surprise might not be the best way to describe Paul's likely reaction.

She had thought Paul had wanted children as much as she did, but after their marriage it became clear his focus was his career, and that he thought hers should be as well. Whenever she'd brought up having children, he'd always change the subject, or nuzzle her neck and tell her they were so good together, why would they want to ruin a good thing? It bothered her and had for a long time. She'd just never found the courage to take a stand. Looking at the positive pregnancy test, she knew the time had come. *They'd just have to deal with it,* she thought, shrugging. Once he got used to the idea, he'd be as happy as she was.

Emma looked at the clock, wondering how she would deliver the news. Luckily, she had an hour before he got home to think of something. She changed out of her skirt and put on jeans, determined to make his favorite dinner—chicken cordon bleu. After a wonderful dinner she'd just tell him he was going to be a father.

As she walked toward the hall she passed the full-length mirror on their closet door. Unable to resist, she stopped and pulled her shirt tight over her still flat belly. *Not for long,* she thought, the happiness coursing through her. All her fantasies of being a mother bubbled to the surface. *Paul will be happy,* she told herself. *How could he not be?*

Thinking of his mischievous smile before he left this morning, Emma knew he had something wonderful planned for their anniversary, but she doubted he could top the gift of a child. Emma laughed softly to herself. It will be okay. We love each other and we'll share that love with a child. But just in case, she hurried to her cupboards to get started on the chicken cordon bleu.

℘

Paul James glanced at his watch, then ran his hands through his hair. He'd been going over the DiChesney file for the last two hours, and he was beginning to get a headache. The state had some airtight evidence on DiChesney that was going to be hard to rebut. *It'll be a difficult case, but I will win it,* Paul thought fiercely. *Even Carrington sees my talent.* He tapped his pencil on the desk, making a checklist for himself of everything to be done before the hearing in two days. *Hopefully we'll get a sympathetic judge.* He made a note to check on that tomorrow.

He went over his preliminary game plan one more time, knowing this case could make his career. With everything seemingly in place, he shut the file and stood to put on his suit jacket. He slid his arms in and felt for the jeweler's case in the jacket pocket. He couldn't wait to get home and tell Emma about his raise and to give her the diamond necklace nestled there in the pocket. It felt good that he was able to give her nice things. He had provided a great living for them before, but with this raise they'd soon be able to take that trip to France she'd been dreaming about.

Paul shut his computer down for the day and grabbed his

briefcase. Suddenly he couldn't wait another moment to be with her. He jangled his car keys.

"'Night, Steven," he called to the man in the next office.

"'Have a good evening, Paul," Steven replied. "Going home for dinner? I think that's a first for you."

"Yeah," Paul said, feeling a little sheepish. "It's our first anniversary."

"Congratulations," Steven called to Paul's retreating back.

"Thanks."

Paul walked through the parking lot of the law firm, whistling as he went. Tonight he would take Emma to her favorite Italian restaurant and give her the necklace. He tapped his suit jacket pocket one more time to reassure himself it was still there. He'd just been able to pick it up this morning from the jeweler. The string of diamonds had caught his eye and when he'd looked closer he could see it made the shape of a delicate heart and hung on a thin gold chain. It was beautiful, and he could imagine it nestled at Emma's throat, catching the eye of everyone in the room.

He fished his keys out of his pocket and climbed into his car, starting the engine quickly to get the heater going. *Arizona may be known for its warmth,* he thought, *but it can get chilly.* He waited a few moments for his little car to warm up before easing out of the parking stall. That was another thing they would be able to afford now—a new car for both of them. Paul turned on the radio and a love song crooned from the speakers. Smiling, he thought of Emma. Her long brown hair, her bright smile, her thin waist and long legs. She was the perfect package.

Traffic was light and before long he pulled up in front of their home in Mesa. He walked through the front door and dropped his keys on the hall table. "Em, I'm home," he called.

She came out of the kitchen, wiping her hands on a dishtowel. "Hi, honey," she said, offering her face to him for a kiss.

"You don't look like you're ready to go. I have reservations at Riazzi's tonight." He followed her back into the kitchen. "Is that chicken cordon bleu I smell?"

She smiled. "Yes, I thought we'd eat in tonight."

He turned her around and swept her into his arms. "What's going on? Am I missing something here?"

Emma gently touched his face, tracing his jaw line. "I have a surprise for you."

Paul bent his head and softly brushed her lips with his. "Me too." He kissed her again. "You're going to be so happy."

She broke away from the embrace. "Everything's ready, so let's sit down."

Just then the phone rang and Emma went into the kitchen to get it. Paul sat down at the oak table they'd recently bought, now laden with food and candles. He poured himself a glass of wine, anxious to see the smile on Emma's face when he gave her the necklace. He sipped his wine as he watched her pace back and forth through the kitchen. After a few minutes she came into the dining room and set down the last dish. The candlelight fairly danced in Emma's eyes as she looked at him. "You are positively glowing tonight, sweetheart."

A shadow passed Emma's face before she said, "Thank you."

"Who was on the phone?"

"It was my dad," she said. "He's in Africa and finally got a connection to check in with me. You know how hard it's been for him since Mom died. He has always thrown himself into his job, but with Mom gone he feels more responsible for me. I just wish his job wasn't so dangerous. I'd hate to lose him, too."

Paul put down his wine glass and came around the table to put his arm around her. "Well, at least he checks in with you regularly." He smiled down at her. "Maybe this will help get that beautiful smile back on your face. I was going to wait, but I've wanted to give this to you all day." He pulled the velvet box from his pocket, flipping open the lid.

Emma gasped, the diamonds giving off a prism of color in the candlelight. "Paul, it's so beautiful," she breathed. "How can we ever afford something like this?"

"I got a raise today," he announced proudly. "A big one. Mr. Carrington gave me control of a very important case and he said I have a shot at being a full partner. We can afford a lot more things—such as Paris." He placed the box on the table and grabbed her hands. "Let's go to France. Let's take a trip around the world." He laughed happily, unaware of his wife's nervousness. "Hey, let's buy a yacht and cruise the seas to celebrate!"

Emma's face fell, her grip tightening on his hands. "I'm so proud of you, honey. But I've got an anniversary gift for you myself." She pulled his hands toward her stomach, her eyes starting to glisten with tears. "I'm going to have a baby," she said softly, her voice trembling. "You're going to be a father."

Paul pulled his hands away as though he'd been burned. "You're kidding, right?" He stood quickly. "You can't be serious. We're always careful." He began to pace, then stopped to look at her. "You can't possibly be happy about this."

Emma stared at her toes. "Yes, I am very happy about this."

He kneeled in front of her. "But Em, how can we achieve all our goals and dreams if we're tied down to a kid? Do you really want to be waking up all night to a screaming kid?" He looked up at her, his eyes earnest, his voice changing to the tone of a reasonable, persuasive attorney. "Kids are messy, dirty, and very needy. You're responsible for another person. Just like your dad. He feels responsible to let you know he's okay instead of just doing his job." He stroked her hand. "What would we do with it while you're working? Childcare is expensive."

Emma extricated her hand and stroked his cheek, seeing a positive ray of hope that he was thinking about childcare. "You just said you got a raise."

Paul stood again. "But not to use on some ungrateful kid who will do nothing but cause us heartache, then turn around and say what horrible parents we were!"

"Not all children are like that," Emma said firmly. "And you will be a great father."

Paul looked down at her, his eyes hard. "I don't want to be a father, Emma. I thought that once you got settled in your career you would give up this ridiculous idea of us being parents. We have a great thing going, just the two of us." He pulled her up beside him. "Why would I want to share your attention?" He tried to nuzzle her neck, his hands caressing her waist. "Besides once you have a baby your body will never be the same. And it's perfect." She stilled his wandering hand and pulled away.

"Please try to understand, Paul. I want this child. It was created in love, it's a miracle it even happened. I want to be a mother," she said, desperate to make him understand. "I'm sure once you get over the shock, you'll see. This is a good thing."

Paul stood before her, his back stiff, his eyes boring into hers. "If you insist on keeping this kid, then you'll be a single parent."

Emma swayed. "You can't mean that."

"I mean every word—I do not want a child. You know what growing up was like for me. I always took second place to my parents' careers. I swore to myself I wouldn't put any kid through that situation, wondering if he is important, having to compete with clients and meetings." Paul's look was hard, unyielding. "I have everything I could ever want—a beautiful wife, a great career, and that's all I want. I don't want children. I can't make that any more clear."

Paul strode toward the hall, picking up his jacket. Emma trailed behind him, shocked at the turn this had taken. Opening the front door he turned back to her. "I love you Emma. I promise you that I will be a faithful, good husband that will provide for your every need. I know I can make you happy, but I don't want any kids slowing us down. It's your choice."

With that, he closed the door and was gone.

Emma sank to the floor, the tears stinging her eyes. Did he really mean it? And if he did, could she live without him? She clutched her abdomen. "What am I going to do?" she asked the empty room. Then her jaw hardened. "I won't give you up," she whispered. "I won't."

Finally, she gave in to the tears.

CHAPTER ONE

Kenneth King walked down the steps of the courthouse feeling frustrated. He hadn't given a stellar closing and he couldn't read this jury, two things that rarely happened to him. To make matters even worse, his client was convinced Kenneth wasn't trying hard enough in his behalf and had threatened to fire him. He threw his briefcase into the car and just sat there for a moment, massaging his forehead in an effort to make his headache go away. Practicing law wasn't everything he had imagined it would be.

Running his hands through his hair, he sighed. *I need a vacation*, he thought. The daily pressure was starting to get to him and he couldn't wait to get out of Arizona.

He went back to his office, barely nodding to his assistant Lauren who didn't seem to notice anyway, and shut the door. But before he could open his briefcase, Lauren rapped on the door.

"Come in," he muttered.

Lauren peeked through the door. "Mr. James wants to see you in his office before you leave on vacation."

Kenneth sat up. That didn't sound good. "Did he say what it was about?"

Lauren shook her head. "Nope, but he said it was urgent."

Kenneth tilted back in his chair, hoping this requested conference didn't have anything to do with his vacation plans. His head still hurt and this wasn't making his headache any better. He grimaced and echoed his earlier thoughts out loud. "I need a vacation."

Lauren smiled. "I know, but don't shoot the messenger."

He smiled back. "Have I ever done that to you?"

Rolling her eyes, Lauren nodded. "Many times, Mr. King!"

After she'd shut the door, Kenneth got up and straightened his tie. He might as well get this over with.

∞

Kenneth King couldn't believe his ears. Paul James sat behind his desk nonchalantly offering Kenneth an astronomical raise and hinted that a partnership in the law firm was just around the corner. Everything that he had worked for since graduating law school was about to come true.

The effort it took to hide his reaction was too much and a grin broke out across Kenneth's face. He looked directly at Mr. James, a little surprised that his mood didn't seem to match Kenneth's. He quickly erased the grin and replaced it with the unreadable poker face he'd perfected in his two years of jury trials. "Thank you, Mr. James, it's a great honor to be considered for a partner in this law firm," he said.

"Call me Paul," he said, sitting down in the expensive leather chair behind the desk. "Mr. James sounds so formal." He leaned forward, his face thoughtful. He licked his lips and muttered something.

"I'm sorry, I didn't hear that."

He looked at Kenneth, but seemed to be looking through

him. "Kenneth, I've watched you over the last year and I'm impressed with your integrity. You seem to be a genuinely good person, from what I can tell. And you're a good lawyer. I didn't think I would say this about a former high school English teacher but I think you made the right choice going into law. You're good at it. People trust you and I . . ." His voice trailed off.

"Paul?"

Paul waved his hand. "Sorry. I'm getting off track." He smiled but it didn't quite reach his eyes. "You are being brought into the inner circle, you have every reason to celebrate. This is what Carrington wants for you and I was chosen to tell you." Paul tapped his fingers lightly on the desk. "Mr. Carrington has been impressed with how you've handled your cases. Even the difficult ones have seemed easy for you. Plus, there's a vacancy with Peter gone now."

"That was terrible what happened to Mr. Stone. I never saw that one coming. He just didn't seem the type that would commit suicide," Kenneth said quickly.

Paul didn't reply. He paused for a long moment. "Didn't I hear that your fiancée also committed suicide?" he asked carefully.

Kenneth swallowed. He didn't discuss Miriam with anyone. It had taken the last five years to get over the hurt and shock of her death. "Yes, she did," was all he said. He wasn't about to tell Paul James that Miriam was the reason he'd given up teaching and become a lawyer. That wasn't for public consumption.

"If I remember the rumors correctly," Paul smiled slightly, "you're a Mormon, aren't you?" He waved toward his secretary's desk. "Apparently the ladies are quite interested in your personal life."

Kenneth felt a blush rising to his collar. He knew he'd been the object of some of the gossip at the office, especially after he'd turned down several invitations to dinner and such. "I never mix business with pleasure, Paul. And yes, I am a Mormon. Why?"

"Aren't most Mormons in Utah?"

Kenneth shrugged. "There are members all over the world, but Utah does have a large concentration of Mormons, since the headquarters are in Salt Lake City. In fact, that's close to where I'm going on my vacation."

Paul digested this information. "I wasn't sure if I could ask you this, but since you're going there anyway . . ." Paul took a key out of his jacket pocket. "I need a favor, and from what I know of Mormons, I think you're the man to do it."

He stopped and reached into the top drawer of his mahogany desk for a file. "When you get back from vacation I'm supposed to turn over the DiChesney file to you," he said, pushing it onto the desk. "I've been working on it for the past six years and I want everything in order so you can transition into lead counsel easily. I'm trying to tie up some loose ends . . ."

Paul paused as if he wanted to say more. He steepled his long fingers in front of him, his small brown eyes looking somewhere behind Kenneth as if weighing his words carefully.

Kenneth watched Paul, his body language speaking volumes. Paul was nervous right now. He was staring straight ahead, but his foot was quietly tapping under the desk. It was somewhat of a game for Kenneth to use body language to help him in a profession where being able to read people was very important.

Paul was different, however. He was intensely private, a man who spoke few words, but those words always had purpose and meaning. From what Kenneth had observed over the last year, body language was the only thing that revealed any of Paul's deeper feelings. Whatever Paul had to say to Kenneth it was obviously important to him.

"I want to get a second opinion on something," Paul finally said, "I need you to personally deliver a zip disk to another attorney in Utah."

Kenneth raised his eyebrows. "If this is about the DiChesney case, Paul, perhaps I should look at the file and offer my opinion. After all, you said I would be transitioning into the lead counsel on the case."

"Hopefully by doing this, the case will be transferred over to you smoothly and quickly." Paul's gaze didn't waver, but he clenched his fist. "I just wish I had a little more time with this."

"Why not just FedEx the disk over to him?"

Paul shook his head. "No, I need this delivered personally. I don't know who I can trust anymore. Emma has the connections that I need on this." Kenneth wrinkled his forehead in confusion. What was he talking about? Who was Emma?

Paul pursed his lips and looked directly at Kenneth as if reading his mind. "Her name is Emma James. She's my ex-wife." He stared unblinking at Kenneth, daring him to say anything. "I need this disk delivered to her with no questions asked. Last I heard she'd joined up with the Mormons and moved to Pleasant Grove, Utah. Sounds nice, doesn't it?"

Kenneth stayed silent, and Paul shrugged his shoulders. "That says something for the Mormons, though, that Emma would join them. Emma was always a fairly logical person. I . . ."

He trailed off. "Anyway, when I heard you were taking a vacation to Utah and that you were being groomed for partner it was like the answer I'd been looking for—the perfect opportunity to get this zip disk over to her. Then when you get back we'll all put our heads together and figure out how we're going to handle the case. Okay?" He paused, then stood as if to say the interview was over, his leather chair squeaking at the movement.

Kenneth stood with him, his 6'2" frame dwarfing Paul's

5'9" height. But somehow Paul seemed to fill the office with only his air of authority. "What's this all about, Paul? Should we really be taking the case to someone outside our firm?" he asked.

Paul didn't answer right away. He only leaned over and scribbled an address on a piece of paper. He stuffed the paper into an envelope. Handing it to Kenneth, he bit his lip. "There's the address I have for her. I think it's fairly close to Salt Lake City, if that's where you're going."

Kenneth shook his head. "No, I was planning on going to Orem to see my grandmother. Pleasant Grove is only about a ten minute drive from there, though."

Paul smiled slightly, but his eyes looked hollow. "They started me out with a big raise too you know, then within a year I was a partner. You could say you are following in my footsteps."

He then grasped Kenneth's shoulder, pointing at the disk. "Giving that disk to Emma is crucial. Please don't ask questions, do exactly what I've asked and do it quickly." He looked at Kenneth, his eyes sad. "When you see Emma, could you tell her I'm sorry? And thanks for doing this for me."

Kenneth shook Paul's hand, taking the disk in the other. "I won't let you down, Paul."

As soon as Kenneth left, Paul took a deep breath. "I'm counting on you, Kenneth King."

ॐ

Kenneth went home and sat down at his desk to begin going through the thick case file. It was not routine stuff at all, defending Vicente DiChesney's companies against charges of money-laundering, drug trafficking, fraud, and tax evasion. Several times it looked as if Paul were about to lose the case, but then the judge would throw out some evidence or make some rulings in Paul's favor. It was odd, really, how many times Paul had made a comeback victory. Kenneth looked at the mountain of evidence against Mr. DiChesney and wondered if Paul were really just that good of an attorney or if he was a very lucky man.

Kenneth sighed and got back to work. He had learned long ago that as a defense attorney you didn't judge guilt or innocence. That wasn't his job. His job was to provide the client with the best defense possible. He'd learned that from Miriam. He leaned back in his chair, wondering how the gossip chain at work had found out about it. It didn't matter really—the story had been splashed all over the newspaper. He reached down to his desk drawer and rifled through some papers before he found her picture. Her smiling face looked up at him. Kenneth closed his eyes. It didn't hurt to look at her picture anymore. He was beyond that now. He still wished she'd just come to talk to him that night, though. Maybe he could have helped, maybe not. He'd never know. She just never seemed like a suicidal person to him. *Ever.* Nothing about her death made sense. Nothing except his vow to become a defense attorney and defend innocent people like Miriam.

The cursor on his computer screen beckoned him and he meticulously started to organize the DiChesney file, jotting down notes on a recipe card so he could familiarize himself with the myriad cases that the firm had handled for DiChesney over the years. It surprised Kenneth to see that Paul was the only attorney listed on each case. That was strange because usually a partner in his position would hand over one or two cases to a junior. As he turned the pages he could see the small computer zip disk placed on top of the file folders out of the corner of his eye and it mesmerized him. Kenneth looked at it long and hard, wondering what was on it that would make Paul act so strangely. *Why would he give his ex-wife in Utah the information?* he wondered. *If it had something to do with DiChesney, I should know about it.*

The temptation was too great and he popped the disk into his home computer and began downloading the information. The file was so large that a message came up on his screen indicating that it would take several more minutes to completely download the file. It was late and Kenneth was tired. Looking at that message, Kenneth was about to shut it off and start again tomorrow when the screen suddenly went black, then came up with a page of what looked like just garbled words. Kenneth scrolled down the page and got more of the same. He furrowed his brow. What did this mean? The letters didn't seem to make any sense. Maybe it was some sort of encryption code. He tried to decipher it, and when he couldn't, he canceled the download, realizing the disk was encrypted. He removed the disk and put it in his briefcase.

"Paul James has a lot of explaining to do," he muttered under his breath.

ɛɔ

At that very moment Paul was in Kenneth's office, meticulously going through the computer disks at the desk. But it wasn't being done voluntarily. An angry man was holding a gun to Paul's head.

"You shouldn't have betrayed us! Where's that disk, James? Where would King have put it?" the man growled. "Mr. DiChesney knows you used your security clearance to make a disk. Now you better find it, because we don't take kindly to traitors. Whatever happened to honoring your attorney–client privilege?"

Paul sneered. "I gave up that privilege the second I learned

DiChesney was a partner with Juan Carlos Miera. My loyalty to my country comes before my loyalty to any client."

"Well, all you did was sign King's death certificate. He'll be an obituary by tomorrow. Mr. Miera doesn't like loose ends."

Paul continued searching, and the man grew impatient. "I'm going to count to three, and you better produce that disk."

Paul shrugged. "It's not here."

"I don't have time for this," the man muttered. "You're just wasting my time."

Paul lowered his head, the words echoing in his ears. How many times had his mother told him he was wasting her time? When he'd shown her his straight A report card or graduated from Harvard Law School the only comment she'd had for him was, "Pride goeth before the fall." Was he prideful? He'd known what he'd wanted out of his life and sacrificed for it. *Even my wife and child*, he thought. *But I knew I'd be a horrible father. What I did was best for all of us.*

He felt the weapon move behind his ear. "Were you really willing to give your life for this?" the gunman asked.

Paul thought of Emma, wishing she'd chosen their life together instead of a child, wishing a lot of things about his life had been different. *I'm sorry about everything,* he thought, *but hopefully this makes up for some of it,* and he squeezed his eyes shut.

CHAPTER TWO

Kenneth arrived early at the law firm the next morning. As soon as he gave the case papers to his assistant, Lauren, he'd be free to go to Utah. An entire week with no clients, no judges, no cases. He couldn't wait. He hoped to have a chance to ask Paul more about the disk without giving away that he'd looked at it. The suspense was getting to him and he'd hardly slept last night thinking about it, wondering why Paul was giving an encrypted disk to his ex-wife, and what was really going on. He ran his hands through his hair. "Let's get this over with," he said, sighing softly to himself. "Utah, here I come."

He pulled his 1960 Corvette Sport Roadster into his reserved spot. He'd restored the car himself, from the 300 HP engine to the white soft top. It was his pride and joy. He loved that car and while he knew he had indulged himself by splurging for original parts, it was extremely satisfying that he could afford it, something he never dreamed he could do as a teacher.

The law firm had been good to him, giving him some big cases. In turn, he'd won the cases for them, making it a win-win situation for both. Not long after winning his first case for them, he had received a substantial bonus and bought the original frame for the roadster. After spending every spare moment in his garage restoring the roadster to her original glory, it wasn't long before he was driving his dream car.

Kenneth walked briskly from the parking garage, the Arizona sunshine reflecting off the glass of the adjoining buildings. He waved to Chad the security guard as he strode out of the garage, receiving a stare in return. Chad had just been hired. Kenneth missed his predecessor, George, who loved to chat with everyone. So far, he hadn't gotten a word out of Chad.

He continued down the sidewalk, marveling at the beauty of the building that held the law firm. It was old-fashioned on the outside, but with every modern convenience on the inside. When the firm had taken it over, they decided to maintain the historic integrity of the outside, except for upgrading some of the materials and redoing a small amount of brick work.

Otherwise, it looked pretty much the same as it had when it was built eighty years before. The inside was completely redone, with marble floors, beautiful hardwood doorways and a gorgeous fountain in the middle of the foyer. Everything reflected the company's success, and Kenneth felt gratified that he belonged there.

Something was different today, though. Four police cars were parked in front of the building, and several of his co-workers were standing on the lawn in front of the building.

"What's going on?" he asked.

"We're not sure," a secretary told him. "They won't let us in the building, though."

Kenneth could see Edward Carrington, senior partner in the firm, standing in the lobby, speaking with police officers. Carrington glanced outside and noticed Kenneth. He immediately came to the door and called out, "Kenneth, we need to talk."

Kenneth hurried over to join Carrington, who put a fatherly arm around him and said, "It appears someone broke into our offices last night, and Paul James was found shot to death in your office this morning."

Kenneth jolted at the horrible news. "That doesn't make sense! Do the police have any leads?"

Mr. Carrington shook his head. "We don't know anything yet, other than he was murdered execution style, two bullets to the back of the head. The police are still gathering evidence." He glanced carefully at Kenneth and said, "I know Paul offered you a raise yesterday. We're looking at you pretty closely for partner, did he tell you that?"

"Uh, yes, he mentioned that."

"Did Paul say anything or do anything that seemed odd to you?" Carrington asked.

"No. He seemed tired and distracted about something."

Carrington put a hand on Kenneth's shoulder, and he tightened his grip. "Did he say what?" he asked urgently.

Kenneth gently shook off the hand. "No, he didn't."

Carrington nodded slightly, and then asked, "Were you and Paul working on something?"

"Not really," Kenneth said, clutching his briefcase a little tighter as he remembered the disk Paul had given him yesterday. "I wasn't even supposed to come in today. I just needed to give some case files to Lauren." He cleared his throat, suddenly feeling like he needed to get out of there fast. "If you'll remember, I'm supposed to be going on vacation today. You approved it three weeks ago."

Carrington nodded. "That's right. We have some big cases waiting for you when you get back."

Kenneth hardly heard him. He stared past the receptionist area to the group of officers huddled near his office door. His stomach clenched as he tried to process the fact that Paul was dead. He knew he had to get out of the building before he lost his composure in front of Edward. "If you'll excuse me, Mr.

Carrington, I do need to go. Lauren knows how to reach me if you need me."

Carrington looked at Kenneth's white face, the shock apparent. "Don't worry, we'll get to the bottom of this," he said. Wait here and I'll see if the police have any questions for you."

Kenneth nodded, feeling a little faint. What was wrong with him? *Paul was murdered in my office,* Kenneth reminded himself. That didn't happen every day.

Carrington then walked over to speak with two police officers. Kenneth watched him closely, his air of superiority evident. Edward Carrington's very presence demanded respect. He was tall and a little too thin, which made his facial features stand out. The warm brown tones of his skin hinted at his Spanish heritage and his once dark brown hair was streaked with white. It only added to the feeling that Edward Carrington was a wise man, experienced in the ways of the world—someone to be reckoned with.

The police officers soon took Kenneth aside and spoke with him, but he explained he didn't know why Paul would have been in his office. The officers seemed satisfied with his responses and moved on to interviewing other employees.

Kenneth got out of there as quickly as possible. He weaved in and out of the traffic on his way home, eager to be on his way to Utah. He finally turned into his driveway and pressed his garage door opener. Idling the car in his driveway, he waited for the garage to open, then pulled in. He got out of the car and was surprised as a gust of wind pushed into the garage, rustling the small bushes near the driveway. The air was heavy and humid, signaling a storm was on its way. Dark clouds rested on the horizon.

He moved into the house, flicking on the lights. Everything looked exactly as he had left it. Going into his back bedroom, he grabbed his packed duffel bag on the bed and took it out to the car, then went in to lock up the house. He walked through the back door and moved toward the hall, when he thought he saw a shadow move. He froze as he looked closely at the large picture of a mountain scene on the side wall. The reflection in the glass showed a man just around the corner holding a rifle.

Kenneth turned, immediately running back toward the garage. He heard two rifle blasts and saw the bullets shatter the wall of the garage. He jumped in his car and slammed it into reverse. The man appeared at the back door, and Kenneth pressed his remote button to close the garage door as he spun his wheels in the driveway, the smell of burning rubber in the air.

The man ran forward, crouched down and took one final shot, which ripped through the front panel of the car. Kenneth sped away, taking side streets to avoid being followed. He finally pulled over to the side of the road, taking deep breaths, the adrenaline pumping through his veins. He got out to survey the damage, his heart sinking when he saw the large hole caused by the bullet.

Kenneth was sure the shooting was linked to Paul's death. He didn't dare return to his home. *I've got to get out of here*, he thought. *If someone is targeting the firm's attorneys, I need to be somewhere safe.* He got on the freeway and headed north, but the storm had hit and traffic was heavy and slow. He had planned to let his mother know he was headed to Utah, but then the day had become so crazy. Now he finally gave her a call on his cell phone as the traffic crept along.

"Hey, Mom, how are you?" he asked.

"Hi, sweetie, I'm fine. Listen, where are you?"

"I'm on my way to Utah for my vacation. I'll be back next Monday."

"Are you still going to stay with Grandma Pepper while you're there? You better, or you'll never hear the end of it."

"Yes, I talked to her yesterday." He paused, wondering how was best to explain his situation without scaring her. "Mom, be careful okay? My house got broken into today."

She gasped. "Your house was broken into? Was anything stolen? Are you okay?"

Kenneth remembered his earlier thoughts that everything in the house had looked in order. If that person shooting at him wasn't trying to steal anything, then surely he was the target.

"I'm fine," he assured his mother, pushing his thoughts aside and making his tone light. "I just don't want anything to happen to you while I'm gone. I worry about you."

"You haven't taken a vacation in more than three years, Kenneth. You deserve this. Have a good time, and I'll see you next week."

Kenneth couldn't help smiling. That was his mother—very no-nonsense. "Okay, I gotta go, Mom. See you next week."

"I love you. Drive carefully and take lots of breaks to stretch your legs," she counseled.

"I will, Mom." He hung up as the traffic started to clear out. Kenneth hit the accelerator. The sooner he got to Utah the better.

CHAPTER THREE

Kenneth drove all day, anxious to be in a situation where he'd have time to slow down and think. The monotonous mile markers nearly lulled him to sleep as he drove. To fight the boredom, he tried the radio, occasionally flipping stations until he found an upbeat song he liked. The hours passed by and after a brief stop in Las Vegas, he continued on to St. George, Utah. *I better stop before I fall asleep at the wheel*, he thought. He pulled off I-15 and saw the top of the St. George Temple ahead. He drove around it, then parked in the temple parking lot and dozed for a few hours. At sunrise, he felt refreshed and continued his journey to Orem.

The closer Kenneth got to his grandmother's house, the better he felt. The sight of snow on the mountains reminded him of how much he missed skiing. Thinking of the ski runs these last few weeks had kept him sane. He glanced at the briefcase. Of course he'd have to drop off the disk, but the rest of the time would be spent on the slopes clearing his head and working out the stress of the last two days.

Kenneth raked his hand through his hair and opened the window to breathe in the fresh Utah air. After the warm weather in Phoenix, it was a welcome change. Not to mention he'd hardly taken any vacation time since he'd started practicing law. His thoughts turned back to the disk. Would Paul's ex-wife be able to interpret the code on the disk? Why was it encrypted? Had anyone even told her Paul had been killed? The never-ending questions swirled in his head with no answers.

He was glad to be able to stay and visit with his grandmother. It had been a while since he'd seen her. He smiled at the thought of her. The family had called her Pepper for as long as he could remember. She was a fireball and always had been, but she had her soft side, too.

He turned into Pepper's driveway. The white two-story house looked almost exactly as it had when he was a little boy. *It could use a coat of paint,* he thought absently, evidence of his grandfather's passing, since his grandfather never let projects like that go.

Pepper spied him through the window and came out onto the porch in her apron, drying her hands. "Kenny!"

Kenneth cringed a little at the nickname. She was the only person he allowed to call him Kenny.

He stepped out of the car and went over to hug her. "How are you, Pepper?"

"Well, I'm a whole lot better now that you're here." She turned back to the house, looping her arm through Kenneth's. She gave him the once over. "You look like you haven't eaten in weeks."

Kenneth laughed. "Now, that's the Pepper I remember. You know my mother tries to lure me over to her house for home-cooking every chance she gets. You taught her everything she knows."

Pepper shrugged and smiled sweetly. "Maybe I ought to teach that daughter of mine a few more things. A man can't go around looking like he's starving."

They walked into the house together. It was simply furnished with lots of pictures of Kenneth and his baby sister Susan growing up. The newest pictures of Susan and her wedding to Robert adorned the front hall table. He bent down to look at the picture in the middle. His grandfather and grandmother flanked Susan on one side, and his mother, father and himself were on the other. He could hardly believe it had only been a year since the wedding. Grandpa died six months later, and Pepper hadn't been the same.

Pepper picked up the picture, tracing a finger over her husband's face. "He looked good, didn't he?" she asked softly, a silent tear running down her cheek.

He put his arm around his grandmother. "He was a wonderful man."

She smiled sadly. "Yes, he was. I miss him every day."

Kenneth breathed in deeply, and an apple cinnamon smell wafted to him. Nowhere else smelled like Pepper's. "Smells like you've been baking." He hugged her, knowing she knew he was changing the subject. He leaned back slightly to look into her eyes. "I am glad to see you're doing so well."

She looked tenderly at him for a moment, then stepped back putting her hands on her hips. "I've been baking all day, but not for you. And you should probably call your mother. She'll be glad you're here to check up on me." She turned toward the kitchen. "Let's get you fed."

She softened a little bit, and turned back so he could see her smile and the teasing twinkle in her eye. "I sure am glad you're here. I don't see enough of you."

"Just don't overdo," he cautioned, knowing his grandmother too well. "You know you get cranky when you're tired and Mom would never let me hear the end of it."

She laughed and walked down the hall, still talking. "I hope you like Dutch apple pie."

Kenneth followed her to the kitchen, holding his hands up in surrender. "Okay, okay. I'll eat, call mom and then I have to make a business phone call. Have you ever not gotten your way?" He didn't wait for an answer and took a generous helping of apple pie.

Pepper poked her head into her pantry and came back in carrying several jars. "I hope you like pickled beets," she said. "I can make a nice roast for us tonight."

Kenneth stood, wiping the last crumb of pie from his lips with a napkin, then kissed Pepper's cheek. "That's fine, Pepper. I'm going to go make those phone calls."

Pepper nodded and watched him ascend the stairs. It was good to have her grandson in the house again. She had been heartbroken when her daughter and son-in-law had moved to Phoenix. She rarely saw them anymore. And now with her Jackson gone . . . well, Kenny could help ease her loneliness. Her eyes rested upon the smiling picture of her husband. *I wish Jackson could be here to share it all with me,* she thought wistfully. But if they were ever going to be the eternal family they dreamed about, she knew her children and grandchildren needed her, and she was going to be here for them.

€›

Kenneth drove down State Street, looking for a restaurant called the Purple Turtle. His phone call to Emma James had not gone as he expected. As soon as he mentioned the law firm he worked for, Emma's voice turned icy cold. She had reluctantly agreed to meet him at The Purple Turtle—which she assured him was easy to find.

He spotted the large purple building and pulled into the parking lot, patting the disk in his pocket. The sooner this errand was over with, the sooner he could hit the slopes. He went through the glass doors and scanned the seats. There was a table full of teenage girls, and one woman in a navy blue business suit sitting alone, her brown hair coiffed perfectly and clipped to the back of her head. He headed for her.

"Hi, I'm Kenneth King," he said, extending his hand. "Are you Emma James?"

The woman turned to greet him and he looked down into the largest brown eyes he had ever seen. She nodded at his question. "Yes, I'm Emma James. What can I do for you, Mr. King?"

Kenneth took a moment to gather his wits, suddenly speechless in front of this perfectly put together woman. Her skin was almost luminescent it was so creamy. *I bet it's soft, too,* he thought, before chiding himself. *You've seen your share of beautiful women.* He mentally shook himself as he sat down, putting on his game face while he pulled out the disk and slid it toward her on the table. "As I explained on the phone, I work at the same law firm as your ex-husband Paul James, and he asked me to give this to you and no one else."

She shrugged, her petite shoulders rustling the fabric of her jacket. "What is it, and why would Paul want me to have it? We haven't spoken in years."

It seemed obvious that she didn't know about her ex-husband's death. Kenneth tried to gauge what her reaction might be to the news since she gave off an air of fragility. He decided to just tell her.

"As I said, I work with Paul and . . ." Kenneth took a deep breath and plunged on. "Not long after he gave me this, he was shot to death," he said softly. "I'm sorry."

At first Kenneth didn't see any reaction in her face, but on closer inspection he could see her jaw working, a small beauty mark near her mouth slightly moving. After a moment she dropped her eyes to the table and reached her hand toward Kenneth. At first he thought she was going to take his hand. *Maybe she needs my comfort,* he thought.

Instead, she reached for the disk and fingered the small, hard object, not looking at Kenneth. She finally lifted her face and brushed a lock of hair out of her eyes, staring at him, her eyes intense, betraying her feelings. "What is on that disk?" was all she said.

"Well," he began, "I think it's encrypted. I wanted to ask Paul about it, but . . ." His words hung in the air.

She dropped the disk to the formica table, lifted her chin and looked him directly in the eye. "Mr. King, my ex-husband was a vain and selfish man." She jabbed her finger toward Kenneth's sports car. "Material things were everything to him. From the looks of it, you two are cut from the same cloth. I don't want anything to do with the disk, or you."

Kenneth was taken aback by her assessment of him. She knew nothing about him! "Hey," he started, but she didn't let him finish. She got up to leave, obviously in a hurry, but Kenneth held her arm. "Aren't you curious about what it is?"

Looking down at him, her brown eyes betrayed sadness. "Like I said, I haven't had anything to do with Paul for over six years. I'm not about to start now." She turned and walked away. Before she could get to the door, Kenneth called out, "He said to tell you he was sorry."

She only paused briefly before continuing through the door, not looking back. Kenneth watched her get into a tan Camry and drive away. Cursing softly under his breath, he put the disk back in his pocket and followed suit. This was not going at all like he had planned. What was he supposed to do with the disk now?

CHAPTER FOUR

That evening Kenneth made his way through the church parking lot, driving as carefully as possible so he wouldn't knock over the little tarts on the trays arranged in star patterns. Apparently his grandmother was in charge of refreshments for the Young Women's Meeting and she'd needed his help in transporting them. He drove around the church once in his search for a parking space, noticing how all LDS churches sort of looked the same no matter where you were, with well-kept lawns and sturdy yet beautiful exteriors. It always felt a little like coming home. He turned his attention back to his task since it didn't look like finding a space was going to be easy. More cars were behind him with the same mission of finding an open parking space. With all the boys running around in uniform it looked like there was also a Scout activity at the church as well as the Young Women's meeting. Kenneth finally ended up easing his car into a space near the garbage bin, far from the door.

He maneuvered the tart trays out of the car and into the church, grateful for the freshly shoveled walks. Gingerly he held the door open with his foot, while still balancing three trays of small tarts. Young boys were practically dancing down the halls, making him even more worried about his precious cargo. He walked down the hall carefully, glancing down to make sure the tarts weren't slipping. His stomach rumbled reminding him that he hadn't eaten dinner yet. He was sorely tempted to take just one of the tarts, but they were in a little star-shaped design, and Pepper would notice one missing. He'd never hear the end of it if she found out. She was immensely proud of her cooking abilities, and took every chance she could to show off a little. He shifted the food in his arms and leaned down to open the door to the kitchen. A young girl about five was sitting on the counter eating a pickle from the vegetable tray, and she smiled curiously at him when he walked in.

"Well, hello there, little lady. How are you?"

Her deep brown eyes just stared at him, and she said nothing. Kenneth carefully set down his load and leaned against the counter. "Are you here all by yourself?"

She shook her head so hard her ponytail swung back and forth until the tip touched each cheek. She offered him a bite of her pickle, but he declined, noting the pickle juice all around her mouth. The girl reminded him of his little sister, Susan. She was always a messy eater and since Kenneth was so much older, his mother had always made Kenneth help clean up her messes. The memory warmed him.

He grabbed a rag by the side of the sink, got it wet and started toward her. The little girl laughed, knowing that he meant to wipe the pickle juice from her face. She started to scoot back up against the wall of the counter, playfully squealing.

At that moment, the door opened and a taller version of the little girl hurried into the room. Her long hair obscured her face for a moment as she picked up the child. "Can I help you?" she demanded in a low voice as she turned to face Kenneth. "You!" she gasped. "Are you following me?"

Kenneth was slightly taken aback by the fact that Emma James stood before him. He stepped forward, his hand outstretched, but then realizing he still held the rag in it, he retracted.

She quickly put the child down on the counter and gave her a once-over. "Are you okay?" she asked the girl protectively, glancing back at Kenneth. "Who are you, really?"

Kenneth shook his head, trying once more to explain himself, hoping to erase the fear from her eyes. "No, I'm . . ." He was interrupted by his grandmother, bustling into the room with her last tray.

She set the tray down and carefully smoothed her skirt. "Emma, I see you've met my grandson, Kenny." She nodded toward Kenneth and turned back to arrange the trays in the refrigerator, missing the look at the ceiling from Kenneth for introducing him like that. "I roped him into helping me carry all my trays tonight. He just got in from Arizona today."

Pepper went on as if she couldn't feel the tension in the room. She looked at the girl in Emma's arms, nestled against her mother's neck. "How are you today, darling?"

Julia snuggled deeper into her mother's neck, but clearly said, "I'm fine Pepper. Did you bring me a cookie?"

Pepper laughed. "I didn't, but if you come over tomorrow I'll give you one."

Julia smiled happily. "Can I, Mommy?"

Emma's glance flicked quickly to Kenneth. "We'll see, sweetie, okay?"

Pepper took Julia's hand and squeezed it. "You're the most precious thing I've ever seen. I'm going to make your favorite— butterscotch chip cookies, okay? You come and visit me tomorrow." Julia bounced a little in her mother's arms, smiling at Pepper's offer. "Don't you think she's the most precious thing you've ever seen, Kenny?"

Kenneth just stood there, staring at the women, amazed that his grandmother felt comfortable enough with Emma and her daughter to let them call her by his family's pet name. They obviously knew each other well.

"What's wrong, Kenny? You looked confused," Pepper chided. "Didn't you introduce yourselves?" She quickly turned to Emma. "This is my grandson, Kenneth King. He's an attorney in Phoenix. And Kenny, this is my good friend Emma James."

"Pepper, may I ask how you two met?" Kenneth asked slowly, keeping his eyes on Emma, still trying to read her. From the way Emma clutched her daughter she was still a little frightened, and with the pasted-on smile she was giving, she was a little confused, too.

Pepper looked from her grandson to Emma. "We met at a Utah League of Women Voters meeting. When I found out she was an attorney I asked her about some things that were going on with your grandfather's will in probate. We've had some long talks."

She winked at Emma. "It's Career Night for Young Women's and I asked Emma if she'd come and talk about the world of law. Of course I'll be talking about nursing." She turned to face Emma. "What's wrong, dear? You don't look well. Are you nervous about tonight?"

Emma smiled wanly at Pepper. "I didn't realize you were related, I . . ." she stammered, seemingly embarrassed at Pepper's words. She reached for Julia. "Come on, Julia, we'd better wash your hands." She nodded politely at Kenneth, then led Julia toward the bathroom.

Pepper looked up into her grandson's face. "Emma's something, isn't she? She might be tiny, but she's a fireball. Definitely a force to be reckoned with."

Kenneth raised his eyebrows. "You must really like her to let her call you by your pet name. That's usually reserved for family. How close are you two?" he asked, trying to keep it casual. He knew it was a mistake as soon as the words left his mouth.

"You like her, don't you?" his grandmother said gleefully.

He knew she was up to her old tricks again. "Penelope Davis," he warned, using her full name so she would know he was serious. "Don't even think about it. No more of your matchmaking." Kenneth waggled his finger in her face to emphasize his point. "I mean it."

Her nervous laugh told him he had hit the nail on the head. "Kenny, would I do that to you?"

Kenneth rolled his eyes. "In a heartbeat."

She stood on tiptoe and touched his cheek. "It's not good for a man to be alone. After Miriam died I think you closed yourself off to love, too afraid to get close to anyone."

He started to protest. "I can manage my own life."

Pepper sniffed, unconvinced of his claim. "I'm just making sure that my favorite grandson realizes he has options." She pointed toward the door that Emma had just gone through. "Lots of options."

Kenneth started for the doorway. "As if you would ever let me forget," he muttered, wondering what plans she had already made for him.

He walked into the gym where Emma was just being introduced. "Sister James is a new convert to the church and just moved here a few months ago. She's a city attorney for Pleasant Grove, and we're thrilled to have her here tonight," the woman introducing her said.

He watched Emma move to the center of the room and begin her presentation as she discussed how difficult law school had been, but with studying and hard work she had made it through. "It was definitely worth it," she told the girls. "Now are there any questions?"

A girl in the front row asked, "Hasn't the prophet told us we're supposed to stay home and raise our children?"

Emma nodded. "That's true, but the prophet also said to get as much education as you can. I think he said that because this is a difficult world we live in. What if your husband can't work, or you get divorced, or maybe even not even get married? It's better to have an education and a skill that you could support your family if you needed to."

Another girl in the back raised her hand. "Does it bother guys that you're really smart?" A few giggles echoed through the gym.

"Yes, it does seem to bother some guys," Emma said with a smile. "But usually those guys are the ones who are really insecure about themselves, so I don't worry about it."

The woman in charge walked to the middle of the gym where Emma stood. "We'd like to thank Sister James for coming and sharing her insights about her career. Now we'll be pleased to hear from Sister Davis, who served as a nurse during World War II."

Pepper stepped to the center of the room, but Kenneth's eyes followed Emma as she gathered Julia in her arms and walked to the back of the room. He had been very impressed with her presentation. She was truthful about the hard work, but also let the girls know it could be a rewarding career. Her brown hair fell across her face as she whispered something to her little girl, then they left through the side door. Kenneth followed. He made it to the hall, but they were nowhere in sight. He checked the foyer and just as he got outside to the parking lot, he saw her tan Camry driving away.

"This isn't over yet," he murmured, wanting to talk to her again. She couldn't get rid of him that easily. Besides, she stirred something in him. Her reaction to the disk was curious and he wanted to satisfy his curiosity, but the way she held herself tonight, the way she protected her daughter and stood up to him, he admired her and wanted to get to know her better.

Or at least have her get to know me better, he thought, *and not judge me by my car.*

He went back into the gym just as Pepper was relating how she met her future husband as a wounded soldier. He'd heard the story many times, and while it was familiar, he always loved hearing his grandmother tell it. It was easy to see how much love his grandparents had shared just by watching her eyes when she talked about him.

"I was in the nursing corps of the United States Navy and was assigned to the USS Comfort, a hospital ship for our troops. We were off the coast of Okinawa in April of 1945, and were loading many wounded soldiers. One, in particular, caught my eye. He had been wounded in the leg, and even though his injuries were serious he insisted that we treat the other men in his platoon first." Pepper dabbed at her eyes. "He was so handsome and brave and I looked forward to seeing him each day. It seemed like we could talk for hours. Unfortunately, it looked like his leg wound had an infection and he would have to have more surgery. I prayed so hard that day because medicine back then was nothing like it is now. Not only that, but enemy planes had already attacked us twice and we were all nervous."

The room was silent. "Well, what happened?" one girl finally blurted out.

Pepper's eyes were far away as if she was reliving that day. "It was the end of April and he was on his way for surgery. I said I would see him later, and he pulled me toward him and kissed me! I floated through the rest of my shift. Everyone was nervous because we had been on a general air raid warning through the night, but all I could think about was Jackson, praying he would keep his leg, that all would be well. We were on our way to Guam and almost there, so everyone was breathing a sigh of relief, but all of the sudden the ship shuddered and heaved. There was fire everywhere and I knew we'd been hit." The girls silently watched Pepper fight to keep her composure. Finally she continued, "I was frantic when I heard the surgery had been hit and most everyone there had died. Jackson should have been in recovery, but I wasn't sure, and with all the commotion I had to use all my skills as a nurse just then. I couldn't look for him for almost four hours. I was so relieved to see him hobbling around, helping other people to their beds. I cried and fell into his arms. I knew then I never wanted to be separated from him again. We were married for fifty-eight years before he passed away."

She looked around at the young women. "If I hadn't been a nurse serving my country, I wouldn't have met the love of my life, so I am very grateful for my education and career. Do you have any questions?"

"What happened to the ship you were on? Did it sink?" a girl in the front row asked.

"No, we didn't sink. A suicide plane had crashed into the ship, penetrating two decks. It went right into the surgery room, which was filled with patients, nurses, doctors and staff. Six nurses were killed, including two of my best friends." She smiled wistfully. "They were dedicated nurses and I'll always remember the times I had with them. But the ship made it to Guam, where it was repaired so we could make it back to the U.S."

"What's the worst thing about being a nurse?" a girl from the back called out.

"Well, not being able to help someone and watching them suffer," Pepper replied without hesitation. "I loved being able to make people feel better. That was why I wanted to be a nurse."

Kenneth walked out, his eyes misty at the recounting of his grandparents' meeting. He hoped she had that written down somewhere for posterity. He hadn't realized that her career had meant that much to her. What did his career mean to him? He thought of the disk in his pocket. That question would have to wait until this whole mess with Emma James was over.

CHAPTER FIVE

Emma wiped the sweat from her forehead, scrubbing the last tile in the bathroom. The two bedroom house had been a great deal because it was a fixer-upper and she had been confident she could do most of the work herself. It had seemed so perfect for her and Julia. She had searched forever in Pleasant Grove, and felt like she'd seen every two bedroom house ever built, including the rat-traps and the ones that were practically mini-mansions.

She sat back, remembering when she had first seen this house. When the real estate agent had ushered her through the front door, she had known it was the one. Once she saw the living room, she immediately fell in love with the bay window and old-fashioned alcoves. Further back to the kitchen, the counters and shelves were a cheerful yellow. Emma hardly noticed the chipped paint and cracked tile. Everything seemed as if it was built just for her so she could finally have a home of her own instead of an apartment. Down the hall was the laundry room and across from that was a room for Julia. Further down was the bathroom and just beyond that was Emma's room. It wasn't a rat-trap or a mansion, but it was just fine for the two of them. And the best part was, it would be all hers. She had closed the deal on the house as quickly as possible, and moved all her things, ready to start her new job.

She knew the house needed new paint, carpeting and tile, and more than a little cleaning. She hadn't realized how much work it was going to take for just one person to do. She sighed.

I'm going to do it, she told herself. Even if it took a little time, she could do it. As she hunched on all fours to finish her task of cleaning away the years of dirt and grime that had collected, she felt the familiar pressure of her daughter climbing the back of her legs.

"Julia, get off, you're hurting Mama."

"Mama, play with me." She tried to wiggle onto Emma's back as if to ride a horsey.

"I will in just a minute. I'm almost done."

"That's what you said when you were on the computer," Julie complained. "I want to play a game."

Emma sat on her haunches and rolled her neck. It had been a long morning. For some reason her computer had frozen on her and she couldn't fix it. She'd spent half the morning trying because she had briefs that needed to be filed in two days and she absolutely needed that computer if she didn't want to go in to work on Saturday. She'd finally given up and took her frustration out on cleaning the bathroom. It wasn't working.

The doorbell rang, causing Julia to jump down and run for the front room.

"Don't open the door, Julia. Wait for Mama," she reminded, slowly getting up off her knees and catching a glimpse of herself in the mirror. She stuck her tongue out at her reflection, trying to smooth her hair at the same time, knowing she was not presentable for company.

When Emma finally made it to the door, she looked through the peephole and heaved a sigh, more annoyed that she cared how she looked than at the unexpected visitor. She grimaced, wishing she had time to at least put some makeup on. Putting barriers between her and Kenneth King was becoming a necessity for her, even small ones like makeup. He was too much like Paul and he brought too many emotions to the surface. She swung the door open.

"Good morning," she greeted Kenneth as crisply and professionally as she could possibly muster.

He was staring at her and she grew uncomfortable under his gaze, knowing she did not look like the polished businesswoman he had met yesterday. Her long brown hair was pulled into a ponytail that was probably crooked, her face was bare of makeup, and the red flannel shirt was two sizes too big, covering denim overalls. And she was holding the yellow gloves she'd worn to scrub the bathroom. The whole situation exasperated her, especially when he looked like he had dressed carefully. She stared back at him, not giving him the satisfaction of seeing her discomfort. She gave him a once-over, from his cream-colored Dockers to the dark brown button-up shirt peeking through the red, expensive-looking jacket that wasn't quite zippered up the whole way. *Why wouldn't he dress well?* she asked herself. *He was just like Paul—always ready to make an impression.*

Well, she had a lot of work to do today and wasn't in the mood to play along. Emma drew her brows together and pursed her lips, hoping to convey to him that she was very busy and his interruption was not welcome. To her surprise he laughed. "You don't give an inch, do you?"

Emma dropped her hands to her hips about to say something about his rudeness but he only laughed harder. She followed his eyes to Julia who stood beside her mother looking every inch like a miniature of Emma. She was mimicking Emma's stance with her hands on her hips, looking very cross. Emma couldn't help it—she laughed, too.

She could tell he was trying to regain control of himself and when his laughter subsided he managed to apologize.

"I'm really sorry. I shouldn't have laughed, but when you. . ." He looked at her pointedly and then at Julia.

Emma let a small laugh escape her lips, breaking the tension. "I know, but when you were looking at me, I decided to give it back to you because I knew I looked awful and you were being so presumptuous." She stared down at her daughter. "Julia loves to copy me. Kids are great at copying adult behavior, good or bad." She ruffled Julia's hair. "You're not exactly catching us at our best."

"First of all," he said as he leaned closer. "You could never look awful," he winked at Julia. "And I am sorry for being presumptuous, it's just. . ." he started to apologize offering her his hand at the same time.

Emma smiled and shook it, hoping the handshake conveyed the confidence she wasn't feeling. "Let's start over again, shall we? What can we do for you?"

Kenneth pointed toward her yard. "I just finished shoveling my grandmother's sidewalk and thought maybe you could use my services here in Pleasant Grove. Besides, we really need to talk." He wasn't about to tell her his grandmother had suggested he do her walks then head over to Emma's. When he said he didn't know her home address, Pepper had pulled out a paper with the address ready and waiting.

Emma looked down at his clothing. "You've been shoveling walks dressed like that?" she asked pointedly.

Kenneth looked down. "What's wrong with the way I'm dressed?"

She just nodded. "I thought as much." He *was* just like Paul, and even though she had been confident in her assessment, she felt a little disappointed. "Thank you for asking, but I can take care of my own walks."

Kenneth felt her demeanor change and wondered why. What did his clothes have to do with anything? He shrugged. "I have no doubt of that." He looked her over once again, and smiled as a blush crept up her cheeks at his obvious appraisal. He turned to walk back down the steps, but didn't get far before he faced her again. "I'll be back later today so we can talk."

"There's nothing left to talk about. I said everything I needed to say yesterday," she replied, looking at her daughter.

"I disagree," he said mildly. "I think we can resolve our little, um, situation, if you'll just listen."

Emma thought of all the things she still had to do today, but having visions of him returning to talk to her, pestering her until she relented. "If I let you shovel my walks will you go away?"

"If you let me shovel your walks, I'll take you two lovely ladies for an early lunch at Pepper's." He winked at Julia again, who rewarded him with a smile. "She was making butterscotch chip cookies when I left."

"Can we Mommy? Please?" Julia pleaded.

Emma's eyes betrayed her anger at Kenneth for using her daughter. "Mommy's very busy today, sweetheart."

"You've been busy all day already," Julia accused. "Do you know how to fix computers?" she asked Kenneth soberly.

He bent down to her level. "Why? Is yours broken?"

"Yes, and Mommy has been working a long time on it and won't play a game with me," she reported.

Emma rolled her eyes. "It's fine, really."

"I *am* really good with computers, if you want me to look at it."

Emma looked down at her daughter's pleading face. "Okay," she surrendered. "It's right through here."

They walked into the living room to her computer desk. The frozen prompt was evidence of the problem.

"Did you try rebooting?" Kenneth asked.

"Yes. I haven't gotten anywhere."

Kenneth tried a few other keys, wiggled the cables, and then rebooted, attempting to "unfreeze" the frame. When it started blinking again Emma almost jumped for joy. "Thank you," she breathed. "I have two briefs that need filing Monday and I really needed my computer."

He shrugged. "No problem at all." Kenneth started for the door and Julia and Emma followed him.

"Thanks again," Emma said and she put her hand on the doorknob.

"You girls get ready and after I'm done with the walks, we'll go to Pepper's."

"Will we go in your little car?" Julia asked. "It looks like a toy car that my friend Nathan has at his house."

Emma shook her head immediately. "We'll drive in our car, Julia."

Kenneth nodded, waved and started down the sidewalk. Emma sighed and closed the door, but went to the window to watch Kenneth shovel for a moment.

He was the complete opposite of Paul in the looks department. Kenneth had dark hair, that curled a little at the back contrasting with his red jacket, and his facial features were more chiseled. *Sort of like a model,* she thought. Paul had been a deep blonde, with a slightly upturned nose. She put her hands in her pockets. It was hard to believe he was gone. But the reality was, she hadn't felt anything for him in a long time. His abandonment had been complete and any love she once had for him had died. She pushed her hair back from her face. She couldn't think about this now.

Julia ripped back the curtains, revealing her mother's hiding place. "Is he done yet? Is it time to go?" she asked loudly, looking out the window. Kenneth had noticed the movement and looked up, catching Emma looking at him. She reddened with embarrassment and pulled Julia to her room.

Emma kneeled in front of Julia and hugged her. "I'm going to change, my clothes, you silly imp, but remember we can't stay long. I've got a lot of work to do today." She thought of the house, the grocery shopping and the briefs that still needed to be prepared, but her daughter came first. *Anything to get this over with,* she thought to herself, chuckling at her rambling. *Thank goodness for Julia.*

CHAPTER SIX

Kenneth finished with the walks, his normally inquisitive mind working overtime on the implications of that disk. What did it mean? Why didn't Emma want it exactly? He sighed, reminding himself he was on vacation and wasn't going to even think about work. He needed to get on the slopes. There wasn't anywhere in the world that had better skiing than Utah and nothing cleared his mind more than flying down the slopes.

He glanced back at Emma's house. His grandmother's new friend was becoming more of an enigma. He smiled as he thought of her reaction to his offer of help. It was obvious she didn't like him and seemed to be holding something against him. What hadn't made sense was her watching him from the windows. *But at least she is watching,* a little voice whispered in his head. *That's always a good sign!*

He walked up to the door, but before he could knock Julia had opened it and was flying down the steps. "I'm ready," she sang.

Her mother followed more sedately behind. "We can't stay long, Mr. King."

Kenneth held up his hands. "I just need a few moments of

your time, and Pepper really did want to see Julia today."

"We'll follow you over," she instructed as she buckled Julia in the backseat.

Kenneth drove down the hill to 300 East, then turned onto State Street. He kept checking the rearview mirror, making sure she was behind him and hadn't changed her mind. When they stopped for a stoplight he watched her smile and look back at Julia, revealing a flash of white teeth. Her high forehead was accentuated with her hair being pulled back. She was a beautiful woman, and Kenneth wondered what had gone wrong between her and Paul. From her comments the day before, it didn't sound pretty.

He pulled into Pepper's driveway and saw his grandmother watching for them out the window.

Emma and Julia pulled in behind him and Julia ran up the steps. "Pepper, I'm here," she called, entering the house.

"So I see," Pepper said happily. "Come look at what I've got for you in the kitchen."

Kenneth watched his grandmother disappear into the other room with the little girl and ushered Emma toward the living room. "I think I need to explain something to you."

Kenneth sat down on the Victorian camelback love seat and Emma perched on the edge of a matching chair, as if she needed to be ready to leave at any moment. "I'm listening."

"This disk seemed very important to Paul. He said he needed a second opinion on a case that he was working on and that he didn't know who he could trust to get the information to you. He was acting strangely, saying you had connections he needed and asked me to give the disk to you and no one else. The very next day he was murdered. I think looking at the disk is the least you could do." He stopped, gauging her reaction. "At least we could satisfy my own curiosity. I probably shouldn't have looked at it, but it was encrypted anyway."

He watched Emma's body language, but she held herself still, not giving anything away.

"Okay, Mr. King. I will take the disk and look at it. If there's anything on it you should know about, I'll give you a call," she said.

"Actually, there are two problems. The first is how will you read an encrypted document, and second, I'd like to be there when you look at it," he said, leaning toward her. "It is a sensitive case for my firm."

Emma sighed. "Okay, you can be there. I have the Xenon decryption program on my computer at work. We can look at it there." She looked at her watch. "Why don't you bring the disk to the city office buildings this afternoon and I'll meet you there."

Kenneth furrowed his brow. "You have a decryption program on your computer?"

"It's a long story," Emma replied.

"I'd like to hear that sometime." Kenneth shook his head. "Should we meet around four then?"

Nodding her head, Emma stood just as Pepper came into the living room carrying a tray. She smiled at both of them. "I made you some hot chocolate."

"Pepper, I really have to be going, I've got a million things to do today."

"Nonsense, you work too hard and everyone has time for a cup of hot chocolate," Pepper chided. "Besides, Julia is not done with her lunch and I told her she can't have a cookie until she finishes every crumb of her sandwich."

Emma relented and sat back down. "Okay, but just for a little while. I really do have a lot to get done today." She sipped her hot chocolate. "How long are you in town, Mr. King?"

"Are you sure you won't call me Kenneth?" he asked.

"Kenny is here for the week is all," Pepper supplied. Emma

nodded. "So, Kenny tells me that you are his boss's ex-wife?"

Emma sputtered, and spilled a small amount of hot chocolate on her pants. "Oh," she said, standing up quickly. She put her drink down on the table and rushed into the kitchen. Both Kenneth and Pepper followed, but Kenneth made it to the sink first, getting Emma a damp washcloth and trying to wipe the chocolate off her pants.

"Sorry," Pepper apologized. "I shouldn't be so blunt."

Emma looked mortified at Kenneth wiping off her pant leg and snatched the washcloth away from him. "It's okay. I shouldn't have worn my linen pants." She glanced over to the table and saw Julia finishing off her cookie. "Julia," she said firmly. "Time to go."

Julia pouted, but brightened when Emma promised to bring her by on Monday after school. "Can we bake something together, Pepper?" she asked.

"You bet we will," Pepper said, ruffling the child's hair. "I can't wait for Monday."

"Me, too," Julia said as she hugged Pepper goodbye. They moved into the hallway where Kenneth was standing.

"Thanks for coming over," Kenneth said to Julia. "See you at four," Kenneth said softly to Emma. "Are the city buildings those small flat ones just past the Purple Turtle?"

Emma nodded. "See you there."

Pepper and Kenneth went out on the porch and waved goodbye. When Emma was out of sight, Pepper turned to her grandson. "So, what did you think of her?" Pepper asked, jabbing her finger toward the direction Emma had taken, trying to be nonchalant.

"You mean Emma? I definitely don't think she likes me, and I think you ruined her pants."

Pepper furrowed her brow. "Really? Why don't you think

she likes you? She's such a friendly girl."

Kenneth leaned forward and closed the door. "I'm sure she is. She's obviously just very busy." He walked back into the living room with his grandmother and sat down, draining his cup, the warmth of the hot chocolate running through him. "She is letting me help her fix a computer problem she has."

"Is that where you're going at four?"

Kenneth nodded. "Hopefully it won't take too long."

He stood up and his grandmother reached up to hug him. "Make sure you're home for dinner with me tonight," she invited. "It's no fun cooking just for myself. I love having you here and I want to hear all about your date with Emma."

"It's not a date," he protested. "I'm helping her with a computer problem, that's all."

"Dinner's at six-thirty." His grandmother said with a smile.

He nodded. "I think I'll take a quick run up to Sundance and get a little skiing in before I have to go," he said and kissed her on the cheek.

ℂ

The man parted the curtains and looked out his motel window, stretching the phone cord as far as it would go. "I've got the address, boss," he said. "I know what to do." He waited for confirmation. "Just get the disk," he repeated the instructions. "I got it, boss." After the fiasco in Phoenix he wouldn't fail this time.

He hung up and put on his black gloves, black jacket and hood. A simple job that paid well, that's what he liked. *Get in and get out. Easy money.* He smiled at the thought. Their intelligence had turned up this ex-wife, and they just had to make sure. He clapped his hands together, then pushed the fingers of the gloves in tight. She wouldn't know what hit her.

An afternoon on the slopes turned out to be just what Kenneth needed. He was a little rusty at first, but after a few runs it all came back to him. By three o'clock, Kenneth's cheeks were rosy and he was chilled to the bone, but exhilarated.

He started down the canyon into Orem, and quickly went to his grandmother's to shower and change. He made it to the Pleasant Grove city building at 3:55 p.m. But Emma was nowhere in sight. He waited until 4:15, and when she didn't show, he headed up to her house. *I hope she's not chickening out on me*, he thought.

Emma pulled into the driveway, exhausted and glad to be home. Grocery shopping with a child was not an easy task and she was late for her appointment with Kenneth. Emma couldn't imagine how anyone with more than one child did it. She had to keep a constant eye on Julia, get the groceries and make sure nothing got in the cart that wasn't supposed to be there. A hot bath and bed sounded so inviting, but she still had to meet with Kenneth, get Julia's supper and had at least four more hours of work ahead of her.

She got out of the car and went around to unbuckle Julia. After Julia's constant questions at the store, she'd had all she could take and planned to get Julia busy coloring at the kitchen table before she went back out to get the rest of the groceries.

They started toward the back door together, Julia chattering all the way about all the things she'd seen at the store and wished she had. Emma was only half-listening, trying to juggle the grocery bag and get her house keys out, when she stopped. *That's funny,* she thought, *the back door looks open.* She remembered closing it, but perhaps she didn't slam it hard enough. She pushed the door open and walked inside, unprepared for the sight that greeted her. Her house was trashed. Broken dishes lay all over the floor. Through the doorway, she could see that the living room looked worse.

Emma let the grocery bag slip to the floor. "Stay right here, Julia, there's glass everywhere and it could cut you." She left her daughter standing at the back door and gingerly picked her way through to the hall. It appeared as though a tornado had swept through her home. Pictures, plants and furniture lay everywhere broken and upturned. She started toward the bedroom when she heard a noise.

"It's just my imagination," she said softly to reassure herself. The shaky sound of her voice made her laugh. *This is Happy Valley,* she thought. *Nothing bad ever happens in Happy Valley.* She adjusted her purse on her shoulder, then she heard footsteps. Someone was still in the house! She dropped the purse and started to run back toward Julia, her heart pounding. She had to get Julia out of the house.

She almost made it to the kitchen when someone grabbed her from behind. Her attacker spun her around, screaming, "Where is it?" Before she had a chance to answer or even react, the man slammed his fist into the right side of her face. She stumbled and went down hard, hitting her head on the wall, making lights dance crazily before her eyes. It felt like the whole right side of her body had been flattened.

He hit her again with a fury she had never experienced, and all Emma could think of was to roll into a ball to protect herself as much as possible. He grabbed her by the hair with his right hand and was choking her with his left hand. "I don't have anything you want," she croaked out.

"That's where you're wrong," he said with a laugh. "We've got some business to attend to." He began dragging her back toward the bedroom as fast as he could. She tried to twist herself free, but he just yanked her hair even harder and dug his fingers into her throat. She was starting to pass out and she knew she didn't want to get to the bedroom, but the doorway loomed closer and closer. Her mind was foggy from lack of oxygen and she wondered where Julia was. Maybe he would just leave Julia alone if she did what he wanted.

Her thoughts were getting fuzzy when a clear image of Julia popped into her mind. She said a quick prayer in her heart, "Heavenly Father, please help me." With that, a primal scream rose from the very core of her being. Using the last ounce of energy she had, she forced the sound past the grip he had on her throat and screamed as loud as she could.

෨

Kenneth pulled into Emma's driveway at 4:25, feeling frustrated at seeing her car there. *Was she planning to stand me up?* he wondered. He turned off the engine and went around to the front door, when he saw a movement on the small porch. He strode up the stairs, surprised to see Julia hiding in a corner.

"What are you doing here?" he asked. "Where's your mother?"

He reached for Julia under the chair and she came out willingly. Tears coursed down her face. "Mommy's crying," was all he could make out between her sobs.

Kenneth arranged Julia's arms around his neck and raised his hand to knock when he heard a terrified scream. He quickly put Julia in his car. "Stay here," he commanded, and ran around the side of the house, taking a cursory check of the windows and seeing that the back door was open. He walked through it into the kitchen and was stunned by what he saw. The entire kitchen had been torn apart. He pushed down his fear, knowing something was terribly wrong. He stepped over the broken dishes, his stomach in knots, wondering where Emma was, and if it was her that screamed.

"Emma, it's Kenneth King. Are you here?"

₮

As soon as she let out the scream, her attacker tightened his grip so she couldn't scream anymore. He stopped to adjust his position, covering her mouth with his hand. She was an unexpected, but delightful complication, and he fully intended to take advantage of the situation. She was so beautiful and delicate . . .

"Don't worry, honey," he breathed in her ear, "we're just gonna have a little fun since I didn't find what I was really looking for." He paused, thinking he heard something. He felt her gasping for air, her body using all its energy just to breathe. No other noises came, and he laughed. This was too easy. *The fun is just getting started,* he thought. But fear rose in him when he heard the other male voice, and he threw the woman to the ground hard, waiting for the new arrival to come in. He didn't want to get caught—going back to prison was not an option. Maybe he could just scare off the other guy and finish what he had started.

₮

Emma hit the carpeted floor of the bedroom with a muffled, sickening thud and she felt the blackness all around her, like a protective blanket. Her last thoughts registered Kenneth in the house calling for her. Never had she felt such relief. He must have come to see why she hadn't shown up. Julia was safe!

Mercifully she slowly felt herself lose consciousness. *At least he can't hurt Julia,* she thought, before the blackness consumed her.

഼

Kenneth turned into the hallway, trying to quell the fear in his heart. He walked toward the hallway, crunching over the broken planters, pictures and dishes. Just before he reached the bedroom door, a wiry man rushed at him, knocking him to the ground. He wasn't expecting the ferocious attack and fell back hard with the attacker on top of him. He simultaneously felt his breath knocked out of him and the explosion of the first blow to his face.

He gasped for air and twisted away from the man's grasp. The smaller man was fast, but he was no match for Kenneth's 6'2" well-toned bulk. When he came at Kenneth again, he was ready. Kenneth felt his fist connect with the intruder's cheekbone.

The man picked himself up off the floor in surprise. "You have no idea who you're dealing with," he hissed, flipping out a switchblade as he backed away, watching Kenneth. He bent down and picked something up off the floor, then turned and started running for the door, slipping and sliding over the broken dishes in the kitchen and streaking through the open back door. Kenneth wanted to go after him, but he knew he needed to find Emma.

He didn't have far to look. She was lying on the bedroom floor in a twisted position. He bent over her, looking for signs of life. "Emma, can you hear me? Are you all right?"

Kenneth touched her chin gently. Blood was pooling on the ground near her head. He knew she was hurt badly. He tilted her head slightly to see if he could see where the blood was coming from. She moaned in pain. Panic rose in Kenneth's throat, but he knew he needed to stay calm. He ran to the bathroom and grabbed a towel from the rack and wadded it up. Hurrying back to the bedroom, he pressed the towel to the back of her head hoping to stem the blood flow, even though he couldn't really see from where it was coming.

"Everything's going to be all right," Kenneth murmured over and over, more for his own benefit than for hers. His eye was starting to swell shut and he felt a little nauseated. He grabbed his cell phone and called 911. The operator asked him several questions about Emma's physical condition, but Kenneth barely registered her words.

"Wait a minute," he interrupted. "I need to go outside and get her little girl."

Kenneth found Julia hiding on the floor of his car. "It's okay, sweetheart," he soothed. He carried her back into the house and settled her on the living room couch.

"Stay right here while I help your mom for a minute," he said. "There's glass everywhere so don't get up because I don't want you to cut your feet," he cautioned. He could hear the sirens, and as he quickly moved to the bedroom to kneel beside Emma. Not knowing exactly what to do with Julia, he flipped open his cell phone and called Pepper. After explaining the situation as briefly as possible he asked her to meet him at the nearest hospital. "Julia's going to need you," he said before he hung up.

He was trying to stay calm, but he could see that the entire right side of Emma's face was swelling into something purple and ugly and her nose was bleeding. It made Kenneth's stomach twist with anger when he looked at the damage the intruder had caused. Emma was so small, and her fragility was magnified by the extent of her injuries. Blood was darkening her hair on the side and the towel was also drenched. It scared him that she was still unconscious.

When the paramedics arrived, they took charge by stabilizing

Emma's neck and getting her ready for transport to the hospital. Kenneth never even bothered to ask if he could go with her in the ambulance. He just gathered Julia in his arms and they went.

"What happened to her?" the paramedic asked as he started an IV in her arm.

"I think it's obvious," he answered curtly, his eyes flicking to Julia. This was not the time or the place to discuss what had happened to her mother. He was doing his best to distract Julia, but his thoughts were on Emma and the fact that the injuries she had suffered were starting to look a lot worse.

"What's her name?" the paramedic continued in a dull, matter-of-fact voice.

"Emma James," he answered quickly, running his hands through his hair while he watched them work on her still form. "Is she going to be all right?" he practically whispered, pressing the little girl into his shoulder as her crying got louder.

"We're going to do everything we can to help her," was all the paramedic managed to say before the ambulance came to a stop in front of the hospital. Emma was quickly taken inside and all he could do was watch the medical personnel whisk her away.

A nurse that had been sitting behind the ER admissions desk moved toward him and directed him to the waiting room.

"Why don't I see if I can find another shirt for you to wear, and we'll probably need to look at that eye," she said in a kind voice.

Kenneth looked down at himself for the first time and realized that he had blood down the front of him. He looked back up at the nurse and nodded. "That would be great," he finally said as he moved toward the waiting room. Pepper stood as they came in and Kenneth transferred the child to her.

"What on earth happened?" she asked.

"Mommy was crying," Julia whimpered. "She had lots of blood on her and she couldn't talk."

"Shh," Pepper soothed. "I'm here, sweetheart."

She turned to Kenneth. "I think I'll take her home with me. Call me when there's news."

"I will. But don't open the door to anyone." Pepper looked at him oddly, but nodded.

When they left, he settled into his chair. Kenneth hated waiting. He had never been a patient person, even as a child, and waiting was extremely difficult for him. That was the worst part about being a criminal defense lawyer. Waiting for a jury to come back with a verdict was par for the course in his profession and sometimes that required days of waiting. He grimaced. Anyone who associated with him knew to stay away from him while waiting for a jury to come back. He was like a caged bear. He just absolutely hated waiting.

He looked up at the television that was droning on to no one in particular and realized that the five o'clock news was just ending. It seemed like it had to be much later than that. He glanced over as the double doors opened for the policeman and he watched him approach the nurses station.

The young nurse handed the policeman a shirt that resembled the scrubs doctors wore with a blue ice bag and pointed the policeman in Kenneth's direction. The officer walked toward him with a grim look on his face.

"Are you the husband of the young lady who's been beaten?" he asked in a brusque voice.

Kenneth was surprised at the man's tone. "No, I'm Kenneth King, a friend." Kenneth stuck out his hand. "Did the nurse you were talking to say anything about her condition?"

The policeman's features tightened even more. "Only that they're still examining her. It could be a while. I'm Detective

Moore." He shook Kenneth's outstretched hand. "It looks like you might need some medical attention yourself," he said as he handed Kenneth the ice bag.

Kenneth grimaced, touching his eye. "Yeah, well, you know what they say—you should see the other guy." He put the bag over his eye, and the coolness of it against the bruising felt like a fire was being put out.

"Can we talk?" Detective Moore asked.

"Sure," Kenneth answered. "Just let me change." He turned his back and removed his bloody shirt. He put the scrubs on and crumpled the piece of clothing in his hands.

The detective sat down near the television and took out a pencil and pad of paper. Kenneth settled on the chair next to him. "What do you want to know?" he asked.

"Can you tell me what happened?" the detective asked as he bent his head to write something on a pad of paper.

"Not really," Kenneth twisted sideways in his chair a little so he could see the officer better. "I was supposed to meet Emma at her office, and when she didn't show up I came to the house to see why. I saw her little girl crying on the porch and when I knocked on the door I thought I heard someone in the house screaming. I went around to the back." He paused and crossed his legs. His shoulder was starting to ache. "The door was open, and I could see that the house had obviously been broken into. I entered to look for Emma. The intruder was still in the house and he attacked me. After I punched him, he took off. I found Emma in the bedroom, unconscious and bleeding, so I called 911."

"How long have you known her?"

"Two days."

Did you get a good look at this guy?" the officer asked.

"No, not really. He surprised me." Kenneth creased his brow, trying to recall the details. "He was small and he was muscular, probably 5'8" or so. He was wearing a dark hooded sweatshirt and he had a black or dark brown mask on." Kenneth searched his memory for any other details. "That's about it."

The officer was writing on his pad, then looked up at Kenneth. "I'm sorry to have to ask this, but did it look as if the victim had been raped?"

Kenneth's stomach lurched at the thought. "No," he said slowly. She was fully dressed in the bedroom, he assured himself. "I think he just beat her." Even saying those words sent chills up his back.

The officer's features softened slightly. He put his hand on Kenneth's shoulder. "I have to ask. It's part of my job."

Kenneth let out a breath. "I know, it's just been a stressful day."

"Well, Ms. James was lucky you were there. We've had two other break-ins in that part of town, but no one was hurt like her." His cell phone was beeping and he reached down to grab it. "Mayor? Oh, I didn't know that. Yes, I'm here with the man who brought her in. No, no news yet. I'll let you know."

He hung up and replaced the phone on his belt. "Apparently Ms. James works for Pleasant Grove City and is pretty popular with its officials. They already heard she's here and can't believe what's happened to her."

Kenneth thought of his own break-in, wondering if it was connected to Emma's. It seemed awfully coincidental. But there had been two other break-ins in Pleasant Grove in the past week, so maybe that's all it was. His stomach tightened at the memory of Emma's face.

"Did the nurse say when there might be any news?" he asked, his brown eyes troubled.

"No, but they might have something by now." The two men stood. "If you wouldn't mind letting me know where I could reach you, I might have some more questions later. And you'll have to come down to the station to sign the formal statement."

Kenneth agreed and recited his grandmother's address and phone number to the policeman.

"Thanks," Detective Moore said, "you were a hero tonight."

Kenneth felt the bloody shirt in his hand and remembered the scared little girl in Pepper's arms. He didn't feel like a hero. "I just wish I had been there a few minutes earlier," he said softly.

The officer shook his hand. "You were there, and that's what counts. We'll let you know if there are any breaks in the case. If you like, we can have an officer bring your car over here."

"Thanks, that would be great," Kenneth replied, fishing the keys out of his pocket. "I think I'll wait and see how Emma is doing before I go anywhere. Have a good night."

"You, too," Officer Moore said.

Kenneth turned to the young nurse in charge of the nurses' station. "Has there been any news?" he asked.

"She's still in the examining room. Let me go see how she's coming along." She got up to move toward the examining area. "Why don't you just sit in the waiting room and I'll come tell you as soon as there is any news at all."

Kenneth turned to do as he was asked. Waiting. Again. How he hated to wait, especially in a room that was named for all the waiting people had to do in it. He sighed as he sat down. *I might as well get used to it,* he thought. *This could be a long night.* He took the ice bag and put it over his left eye, then stretched out in a chair to wait.

CHAPTER SEVEN

Emma felt as if something sharp and heavy was resting on the right side of her head. As she became more aware of her surroundings, she could hear people talking and the odor of antiseptic filled her nostrils, signaling to her sluggish brain that she was in the hospital. Her thoughts drifted in and out as she listened to the conversation around her.

"There's definitely a cracked collarbone, and she is going to have a whopping headache," someone said to her left. "At least we only had to put in eight stitches for that cut in the back of her head."

She tried to open her eyes, but her body seemed heavy and unwilling to respond to her commands. She gave it all her effort and her left eye opened to reveal a nurse and doctor standing next to her bed. The nurse leaned over when she saw the eye open.

"Hi there. How are you feeling?" she asked in a soft voice.

Emma tried to speak but it came out as more of a croak. "Not so good," she managed to say.

"Can you tell me your name?" the doctor asked.

"Emma James. What happened?"

"You were attacked in your home this afternoon and were

beaten pretty badly," the doctor said. "You have eight stitches just above the hairline on the back of your head, a concussion, a cracked collarbone, and bruises all over your body. But you should recover fully."

The doctor looked almost happy after finishing his recitation of her injuries, and it annoyed her. *Let's have the shoe be on the other foot,* she thought, *and see how happy he'd be.*

"The police are going to want to talk to you in the morning. I'm going to keep you overnight for observation. Is there anyone we can call for you?" the doctor asked as he leaned over to shine his pen light in her eyes.

Emma tried to sit up. "My daughter, Julia. Where's my daughter?"

The doctor gently eased her back down. "Well, there's a man outside that came in with you. I'll go see what I can find out."

She tried to clear her mind and think of the details. Someone had been in the house. She remembered the footsteps and running for Julia, desperate to get her to safety. The last thing she remembered was hearing Kenneth King calling for her. She relaxed a little.

The nurse smiled as she rearranged the pillows for Emma. "The guy that came in with you has been waiting to see you all evening." She leaned over conspiratorially. "He's so good-looking. I heard he saved you from the attack by scaring the guy off. I wouldn't mind having someone who looked like him watching over me."

Emma felt the tears squeezing out of her eyes, and the nurse looked at her in concern. "I'm sorry. If you're not up to seeing people we don't have to let him in," she said gently.

"No, it's not that," Emma said, "I just... I'm just so grateful he came along. He must have saved my daughter and maybe even saved my life."

"Well, I'll go get him in a few minutes," the nurse replied.

"But for now, let's get you cleaned up a little."

₭

Kenneth looked up from his chair as the nurse came toward him. "She's awake and wanting to see you, but you can only stay a few minutes." Her voice softened. "Go easy on her, and don't act surprised when you see her. Her face is pretty battered. We want to keep her spirits up."

He followed her behind the curtain. He tried to make his face impassive when the nurse stepped aside and he saw Emma. She did look awful. She had one large purple bruise from the top of her right eye down to her chin. Her hair was matted from the blood, making the chestnut brown a shade darker. He looked away—it was almost more than he could take. If he had arrived just a minute sooner, maybe he could have saved her some of this suffering. When he looked up, his eyes met hers and he was surprised to see tears in her eyes. She reached out a hand for him.

"How can I ever thank you?" she asked. "I'm so glad you were there . . ." Her voice wavered as emotion overtook her. He could see how hard she was fighting to keep her composure.

He rubbed her bare ring finger almost nervously. "I just wish I had been a little sooner," he said gently. "I am so sorry."

She looked surprised. "It's not your fault. I saw the back door was open and I should have never gone inside. I guess I was naive enough to think that nothing bad ever happens in Happy Valley." The effort of remembering was starting to make her feel tired. "Is Julia with Pepper?"

At that moment the nurse came in, checked her vital signs and gave Emma some medication. When she was done, she indicated to Kenneth that it was time for him to go.

"Where's Julia?" Emma asked again.

Kenneth stood. "Don't worry about Julia. Pepper took her home."

"Thanks," she murmured softly, the exhaustion really starting to take effect now. "Tell her I love her and I'll see her tomorrow." She closed her eyes. "Thanks for coming for me."

Kenneth felt the protectiveness in him surge and he stroked her hair away from her face, watching her sleep. Kenneth turned to go and almost bumped into the nurse. "How long is she going to be here?" he asked.

"At least overnight for observation," she answered. "You're welcome to come back in the morning. I'm sure she'll be more up for talking tomorrow. The police will be back to question her and they may want to speak to you as well."

"I've already spoken to Detective Moore, " Kenneth replied grimly. "I wish I would have gone after the guy who did this."

"No," the nurse said firmly. "You did the right thing. Ms. James needed medical attention and you got that for her. Let the police chase the criminals."

He looked down at Emma's battered face. "I will help them put this animal behind bars," he said, his voice harsh.

The nurse looked at him sympathetically and put her hand on his shoulder. "You were a hero for her tonight."

They walked back to the desk together and Kenneth continued on through the double doors. He didn't feel like a hero, and he was pretty sure he didn't look like one, either, with the shiner he had earned.

∞

Pepper was waiting up for him when he came through the door. "How is Emma doing?" she demanded.

Kenneth ran his fingers through his hair. "It looks like she'll be fine. Her face is pretty bruised."

Pepper put her hand to her mouth. "It's just so horrible. Did he, you know . . . hurt her?"

"No, she wasn't raped, but that's probably what was going to happen."

His grandmother gasped. He went to her and put his hands on her small shoulders.

"She's okay, and she's got us to help her recover."

Pepper started to cry softly. "That poor girl."

Kenneth was surprised at his grandmother's tears. She was the strongest woman he knew. "Pepper, it's going to be okay, I promise." He hugged her close. "Everything is going to be all right. Where's Julia?"

Pepper returned his hug fiercely. "I know it'll be okay. An old woman is entitled to a few tears now and then you know." She stepped back. "I put Julia upstairs in my bed. She's sound asleep finally. I wonder if she saw everything that was happening to her mother." She started toward the stairs. "I think I'll go to bed. I want to be there if Julia wakes up and is frightened. You ought to get some sleep, too."

He did as he was told and went up to bed, but it was hard to sleep as images of Emma's battered face haunted his thoughts. He went over the scene in his mind, reliving the horror of it and imagining Emma's fear. He felt physically sick thinking about what would have come next if no one had helped her. Even though he'd only known her two days, he felt strangely protective of her. With his mind in turmoil, sleep was long in coming.

The next morning Kenneth woke up bleary-eyed, still tired, and with the worst headache he had ever experienced. He turned over in bed and looked at his clock. Eight o'clock. He sat straight up. He didn't hear any of Pepper's usual clanging about the kitchen, so maybe he could get a little more sleep. Then through the crack in his open door he could see a little figure staring at him. He smiled, but she didn't smile back.

"Are you okay, Julia? Do you want to come in?" Julia shook her head, but crawled forward, opening the door wider.

"Where's Mommy?" she asked, her brown eyes wide.

He sighed. "Mommy's still at the hospital. They're fixing her up. She'll come home today, though. Are you hungry?"

Julia nodded and started downstairs. Kenneth closed the door and quickly changed, putting on some sweats and a sweatshirt before following her downstairs. He came through the kitchen entryway and started rummaging through the cupboards. Glancing back at Julia, he asked, "Do you like cereal?"

Julia shook her head. "I eat oatmeal in the morning. Mommy says that's good for me."

Kenneth groaned. A health nut. He didn't have any clue about how to make oatmeal. He held out the box of sugared cereal Pepper had bought for him. "Doesn't this look good?"

Julia nodded her head happily and climbed up to the table. Her chin rested on the edge and Kenneth rounded up two phone books for her to sit on while she ate. When he set the bowl in front of her, she dug into the cereal with gusto, clearly excited about trying something new. Pepper came downstairs, eyeing the cereal that Kenneth had obviously given Julia.

"She was hungry," he offered in defense.

"Well, that won't fill her up," Pepper countered. "Little bodies need good fuel."

"It never hurt me any."

Pepper snorted and went around to Julia. "How are you today, sweetie? Are you feeling better?" She took her little hands and gave them a squeeze.

Julia nodded, her mouth full of food. "I like Kenny's cereal."

Pepper rolled her eyes. "Emma's going to kill us. I overslept today because I didn't sleep very well last night thinking about—" She glanced at the child. "I'm going to make her something really good to eat."

Kenneth just laughed. "It's good to experience a little of the world. And it won't kill her to have one bowl of cereal."

Kenneth sat down at the kitchen table with his own bowl of cereal, but finished quickly, watching his grandmother go back and forth, eventually taking muffins out of the oven.

"So what are you going to do today?" Pepper asked. "Do you want to visit my ward?"

He shook his head. "I'm going back to the hospital to check on Emma."

"Before you do that could you go back to the house and get some clothes for Julia to wear? Then I can bathe her and she'll have clean clothes to put on."

Kenneth stood. "I better get going then. I'll see what I can find at the house."

When he rounded the corner leading to Emma's back door it was obvious the police had been there. Police tape marked the floor, but since the house had been in such disarray before, he couldn't tell if one policeman had been there or a thousand. He picked his way to Julia's room and found her dresser. He had no idea what little girls liked to wear so he brought two dresses and a few pants and shirts with him.

Pepper oohed and ahhed at the frilly selections, and quickly chose the pink lace dress for Julia to wear to church. Pepper said the little white overalls and pink cotton shirt would do fine for after church. Once Julia was dressed and settled with Pepper happily reading books, Kenneth started back to the hospital to check on Emma.

On his way, he stopped at a flower stand near the hospital and picked out pink roses, hoping Emma liked that color. He pulled into the hospital, and grabbed the flowers he had brought for Emma from the passenger seat, grimacing with pain. Whatever he had landed on when he fell had done something to his shoulder. He rotated it again, wincing a little. His body hurt. His hand instinctively went to his eye and he thought about Emma's injuries. If he was hurting this badly, he couldn't imagine what she was feeling.

He walked up to the information desk to get Emma's private room number. As he neared her room, he saw Detective Moore walking toward him. "Hey, how are you this morning? That eye looks pretty sore," he said.

"It *is* sore," Kenneth replied. "I've had a whopping headache all morning. Do you have anyone in custody yet?" he asked, getting right to the point.

The detective's face darkened. "No, but the disturbing thing is we found her purse with some ID in it in a garbage bin about two houses down. It had obviously been gone through. I brought the item over to her today so she could tell us what was missing." Detective Moore looked at Kenneth seriously. "He took her planner and her keys."

Kenneth's eyebrows knit together. "So," he said. "Everything in a planner can be replaced, can't it?"

"Everything can be replaced, but as of now that creep has her house keys, phone numbers and addresses of everyone she knows. Pretty much her entire life was in that planner, and that man has access to it all." The officer sighed. "He was looking for something in particular. She remembered him screaming, 'Where is it?' but she had no idea what he was talking about. She's worried that he might come after her again."

Kenneth absently rubbed the hand that had struck the man. "Did you check the neighborhood for potential witnesses?"

"Yes, but we didn't receive any substantial leads. It looks like she interrupted a robbery. The weird thing is how badly he trashed the house. He was definitely looking for something." The officer cleared his throat. "The problem is we don't have much to go on. The only substantial evidence we have is the partial fingerprints from the house, some bloodstains, and the purse. Other than that we just have to wait for lab results."

"Have you gone through the database for any felons living in the area? Have you looked at the other two break-ins to see if this is a pattern crime?" Kenneth's voice rose. "It seems to me there's plenty you can do."

The detective was trying not to look annoyed, but Kenneth could see the detective's jaw working overtime. "We're doing our job, Mr. King. The best thing you can do is let us take care of the investigation."

Kenneth certainly didn't want to antagonize the police, but knowing he couldn't do anything was making his frustration level rise. He looked at the ceiling to try and calm down and took a deep breath. "I'm sorry, detective. I just feel like we should be doing something more." He looked the officer in the eye. "If you need anything from me, let me know. I'm an attorney and I'd like to help in any way I can."

The officer looked at him, a little less annoyed than a moment before. "I will, Mr. King. We will do the best we can to find this guy."

Kenneth glanced past him to Emma's room. "I know. Thanks again."

The two men shook hands as Kenneth moved toward Emma's room. He knocked timidly on the door. He could hear her crying softly, which stopped at his knock and she sniffled, "Come in."

Kenneth entered the room with the flowers behind his back. He stepped forward and was unprepared for Emma's gasp of surprise. "Your eye," she said. "I didn't see how bad your eye was last night."

He looked at her sheepishly. "I had been icing it, and it does look a lot worse today. I hope the other guy looks at least as bad."

She stiffened at the mention of the attacker. He mentally kicked himself and immediately apologized. "I'm sorry, Emma. We don't have to talk about it if you don't want to."

"No, it's all right. It's not like we can pretend that it didn't happen. Look at our faces for heaven's sake. We could be twins with the shiners we both have." She gingerly touched the right side of her face.

"Do you feel up to telling me what happened yesterday?" Kenneth asked as he set the flowers on her bedside table next to a large arrangement. "Wow, someone sure loves you," he commented.

"It's from the city offices. They're great people to work with," she said. Emma shifted her legs, looking very uncomfortable as she tried to sit up straighter in her bed. She smoothed the hospital gown and unconsciously brought her hand up to her throat where more bruises were plainly seen. "I hope I never have to live through another day like yesterday," she said. "Julia and I were coming home from the grocery store. The back door was open and when I went in I saw all my dishes broken on the floor. I told Julia to stay there by the door and I went to see the condition of the rest of the house."

She paused and pulled her knees up to hug them. "I heard footsteps and turned to run back to Julia, but he caught me. He was choking me and pulling me toward the bedroom." After a long pause, her emotions won and she started to cry. "If you hadn't done what you did, we all know what would have come next."

"We don't have to think about that because you're safe now," he reassured her.

"How can you be so sure?" she demanded. "Do you know he has my planner? I had everything in there, my checkbook, my work schedule, Julia's sitter information, my extra house keys, everything!" She lowered her voice. "He wanted something, and what if he thinks I still have it? Now he will know exactly where Julia and I are at any time of day. Do you know how that makes me feel?" She wiped the tears from her eyes. "Not to mention he broke the china I'd been collecting since I was a teenager."

Kenneth shook his head desperately trying to think of something to say that might make her feel better. He looked at her tense, shaking body, curled into a ball and gingerly drew her close to him in an embrace, trying to absorb her pain through the contact. He felt self-conscious for a moment, as she didn't relax but remained stiff in his arms. "I'm not sure how long I'll be here, but you could let me help you as long as I'm here. I am great as a nursemaid."

He patted her shoulder awkwardly and released her, since his touch obviously wasn't helping. He turned to cover his embarrassment and poured her a glass of water. "When are they letting you out of here, anyway?" he asked, changing the subject.

The air of awkwardness in the room was increasingly apparent as Emma drew her sheets up before she answered and she wouldn't meet his eyes. "As far as I know as soon as the doctor comes to check me over, I am free to go. I'm just not sure what I'm going to do." She took the offered drink and began to speak as if Kenneth wasn't even there. "How am I going to go to work like this? How can I explain these bruises? And what if he tries something again?" The look of fear was in her eyes, and her voice became emotional. "What am I going to do?"

Kenneth sat on the windowsill, creating some distance between them. "I can help, you know. I'll do anything you need me to do."

Emma closed her eyes. "It's okay. I don't really need anything. I can take care of myself and my daughter," she said.

Kenneth folded his arms. "Everyone can use a friend

sometime," he said softly.

Emma squared her shoulders, and bluntly said, "I'm sure you have better things to do. Aren't you supposed to be on vacation?"

He held up his hand as if in surrender. "Hey, I'm just being friendly. If you'd rather I didn't . . ."

Kenneth saw her shoulders fall and when she looked up her eyes were shining and the bravado was gone. "Actually, I could really use a friend right now."

Kenneth moved over to the edge of the bed. "So what's the first thing on your 'To Do' list?"

"Well, I think when I get out of here, the first thing to do is to start cleaning up the mess in my house and see what can be salvaged. Then, get Julia. Do you think your grandmother could watch her a little longer today while we clean?"

Kenneth immediately picked up on the "we" and smiled his most winsome smile. "Does that mean you are taking me up on my offer to be your personal nursemaid?"

Emma laughed, then winced with pain. "I'm doing you a favor since you look so awful no one else would have you."

"Hey," he protested her remark, as he moved away from her bed. "I'll see if I can't round up a doctor and find out when I can take you home."

She reached over to put down her water and swayed a little when she sat back up.

Kenneth barely caught her. "Whoa, let's not go too fast there."

She smiled wanly. "This is going to take more getting used to than I thought."

He helped her ease back down without hurting her collarbone or stitches. She really did look a lot better today. Her hair had been washed, and she was wearing a support sling on one arm that went underneath her hospital gown for her injured collarbone, but that was hardly noticeable. It was definitely the bruises on her face and neck that bothered him. The ugly purple bruises contrasted so sharply with her fair complexion.

"I'm going to go find that doctor, Emma, and I'll be back as soon as the doctor says you can leave. If you need anything else before then, let me know. I'm just a phone call away."

"Kenneth," she called out before he got far. "Thank you," she said. "I know it's not much, but thank you for everything."

Kenneth turned back. "Anytime."

He went down to the nurses station and got the ball rolling, but it took about an hour to get Emma released. They had all sorts of last-minute instructions for her and papers to be signed. He was thoroughly exasperated by the time they were done.

She just smiled. "You should be used to all this paperwork. Aren't you a lawyer?" she joked.

He laughed back. "I have an assistant to do the paperwork for me," he muttered.

The drive home was short and the conversation centered on Julia. She seemed a little dismayed that he'd given Julia sugar cereal for breakfast, and after a phone call to check on Julia found out that she was making sugar cookies with Pepper as they spoke.

"I try not to let her have too much sugar."

Kenneth grinned and glanced over at her. "I think she really likes it."

Emma groaned. "That's what I'm afraid of. Do you know how much dentists charge these days?"

He drove past the Pleasant Grove City offices and Emma turned to him quickly. "Did you bring the disk with you?"

Kenneth nodded. "Why?"

"Yesterday," she winced with the memory. "The guy said he couldn't find what he was looking for. It got me thinking and very curious about what's really on that disk. That could be what he was looking for. I mean, what if Paul told someone else about it? The city manager's car is in the parking lot, so he could let us in. Let's go take a peek at that disk. I haven't been able to stop thinking that that's what that guy was after," she admitted.

"You just got out of the hospital. Do you think this is a good idea?"

Emma gave him a frown. "I thought you said you wanted to be my friend. Well, the first thing my friends realize is that I know my limits. I can handle this."

Kenneth pulled into the small parking lot. "Are you sure you're up to this?"

Emma was already opening the door. "I'm okay, I'll just take it slow. Don't worry about me," she chided. "I'm stronger than I look."

They crunched through the snow and knocked on the glass. A large man dressed in sweats and a BYU sweatshirt came to the door. "Emma," he exclaimed. "What are you doing here? I heard you were in the hospital." As she drew into the light, Fred gasped. "You look awful."

"Hey, Fred, thanks a lot," she said, grimacing. "What did you expect?"

"Are you crazy? Why are you coming in to work?"

"I'm just going to check one thing and then I'm out of here," Emma said. "The mayor gave me a week off to recuperate, and I'm going to use it."

She turned and faced the two men. "Fred Brandon, this is Kenneth King," she waved toward Kenneth, then fell into step beside Fred. He walked down the hall with her, stopping in front of a large door. Kenneth trailed behind the pair. "Let me know if you need anything," Fred said as he disappeared inside.

Emma continued down the hall, leading Kenneth to a far

corner office. "Here we are," she said, flicking on the lights. Kenneth came through the door, and Emma motioned him to a chair. The room was pleasantly furnished, a large oak desk being the focal point. She sat down in the swivel chair behind the desk and started up her computer. "This should just take a minute. Do you have the disk?"

Kenneth handed it to her and she put it in the disk drive. With a few keystrokes the information was downloading. "So, why do you have a decryption program on your computer?"

Emma smiled. "That's top secret information. I could tell you but then I'd have to kill you," she joked. "My dad is a director in the CSIS."

At his look of confusion, she explained, "The CSIS is a Canadian federal organization that works closely with the Royal Canadian Mounted Police in gathering and analyzing information that would be pertinent to national security. It's sort of like the American CIA. My dad gave me the system so he can e-mail me privately and such. Here we go." She inched forward, looking at what was coming up on the screen.

Kenneth leaned over her. "Look, it's names of clients that we've had." As she scrolled down the page he could see a list of several cases the firm had worked on with the names of judges, immigration officers, local law enforcement officials, banks, and a federal officer. To the right of their names were dollar amounts and dates. Kenneth scrolled down the page and the next list was of businesses in the area, all linked to the Green Credit Service. Beyond that there was a name—Juan Carlos Miera. There was also a travel itinerary to Colorado and a large sum of money.

Kenneth pointed at the screen. "Isn't Miera a known terrorist and arms dealer? What would our firm have to do with him?"

Emma was tapping her fingers on the desk. "I'm going to e-mail this to my dad, encrypted. He should be able to help us."

Emma began opening her e-mail account. "This shouldn't take long to send to him." After the e-mail was sent, Emma began shutting down her computer. "I'll come back tomorrow and see if he answered me."

Kenneth took her arm. "Now I think you need to go home and recuperate."

"You don't have to babysit me," she said, her tone sharper than she intended. Kenneth stopped and put his hand on her shoulder. "I know you're capable, Emma. I just want to help."

Emma felt the anger drain out of her. "I know and I'm sorry. I'm just kicking myself that this happened at all. I know you just want to help and I really am grateful."

They walked down the hall and said goodbye to Fred. Kenneth helped her to the car, his worry increasing when she suddenly leaned heavily on him. "Oh, I'm sorry," she said. "I'm so tired."

"We'll be home soon," he said as he helped her into the small seat of the sports car. Kenneth backed out, turning onto the street that led to Emma's house. She had already shut her eyes and looked like she was sleeping.

They pulled into her driveway, and she looked up groggily. "Here already?"

Kenneth nodded and came around to her side of the car to help her out. She opened the front door and surveyed the disaster. "This is going to take more than two people to clean," Kenneth commented. "Maybe you should just stay at Pepper's for now."

Emma didn't reply. She gingerly walked over her books and pictures on the floor to her computer desk. The screen was smashed, the hard drive torn out. It was ruined. "Oh," she moaned. "I had so much on that computer that I needed."

"Did you have any zip disks to back it up?" he asked.

"Two, although I don't see them right now," she replied.

"It's tough to see anything through this mess."

Kenneth could see her frustration and said, "Hey, don't worry. We'll get this cleaned up tomorrow."

She turned to him, unable to hold back the tears. "I can't believe this is happening."

He opened his arms and gathered her in. This time the awkwardness was gone. "Shh, it'll be okay, I promise."

She stood there a moment until the tears had subsided. He pulled a handkerchief from his pocket. "Thanks," she said, smiling up at him. "I didn't know guys carried hankies anymore."

He smiled. "Pepper always said a gentleman carries a handkerchief." He took her gently by the shoulders. "Let me take you back to Pepper's house for now. Things will look better in the morning."

She nodded and allowed him to lead her back to the car. She was silent on the way back to Orem. "What are you thinking about?" he asked, watching the road while trying to watch her.

"I'm wondering why Paul wanted me to have that disk," she said wearily. "Paul rarely trusted me with anything. He liked to buy us things, he liked to show me off, but it was more as if I was an accessory, not a person. I can't imagine him giving me something important. I wonder what my dad will have to say about it." She twisted gingerly in her seat. "And what if this guy comes after me again?"

"Right now you need to concentrate on getting better." He touched her hand. "No one is going to hurt you, Emma."

She nodded and let him hold her hand for a moment, then released it and folded her arms across her chest. Kenneth recognized the movement as defensive and knew she was feeling overwhelmed by everything, but he couldn't help it. He wanted to be close to her, to help her through this. She evoked feelings in him he had begun to think he would never feel again after Miriam.

They arrived at Pepper's house and Julia came running out to greet them. "Mommy," she called.

Emma embraced her with one arm. "Sweetheart, I missed you," she said, her eyes bright with tears. "Did you have fun with Pepper?"

"We made pies," she said solemnly. "We get to bring home a key lime pie. Pepper said that was your favorite." She touched Emma's face carefully. "You have lots of owies on your face, Mommy."

"I know honey. It hurts too, but it's going to get better. Don't you worry, okay?"

Emma stood and walked up the porch where Pepper was waiting. "Thank you so much, Pepper. You don't know what it meant to me to know she was being taken care of."

Kenneth joined them and said, "Pepper, do you mind if Emma and Julia stay here with you for a while? It's going to take a little time to clean up their house and make it livable again."

"There's plenty of room," Pepper gushed. "I'll make up the other guest room for you. Come and eat first, though, Emma, then you can go to bed. You look exhausted."

"I've got to get out of these clothes," Emma said. "And I'd like to take a long, hot bath."

"Let's go inside," Kenneth said, steering the women into the house.

After Emma had time to bathe and change, they sat down to Pepper's famous pork chops. "These are so good," Emma complimented. "You are such a great cook."

"It wasn't always that way," Pepper said. "When I first got married I could hardly boil water. I could bandage wounds and make beds with hospital corners, but cooking was not my thing. I learned, though, and Jackson appreciated it. Cooking helps me feel closer to him."

"I appreciate it, too," Kenneth chimed in, between mouthfuls, making the women laugh.

After the meal they moved to the living room and sat talking, letting the conversation flow easily around them. Julia planted herself on her mother's lap on the couch and seemed content to just be near her. It had taken a while for her to adjust to the bruises on her mother's face, but they both seemed relaxed now.

Pepper regaled them all with embarrassing stories about Kenneth when he was a boy, even telling the one about the time when he gave his dog some cold medicine because he thought his nose was running. That dog acted drunk for two days. The vet said the medicine could have killed the poor dog if Kenneth hadn't diluted it in water.

Emma almost choked with laughter. "I think it's cute that you cared about your dog so much. You are obviously a very caring person." *Much different than I thought originally,* she chided herself.

"Well, you wouldn't be saying that if I had killed the dog."

Emma noticed him watching her and it didn't bother her. She felt so content with her daughter in her lap and her friends around her. She tilted her head as if to stretch her neck and winced.

"Are you all right?" Kenneth asked.

She felt embarrassed that her pain was so obvious. "I'm fine. My collarbone is just sore." Her eyes became misty. "I just don't know if the memories will ever go away."

Kenneth's eyes were so sympathetic when he looked at her. "It's going to take some time Emma. It will fade, but it will take time."

Emma felt the tears coming again, feeling his caring. "You've been really wonderful to me. I'm just tired, and I could use another pain pill."

Pepper stood and held out her hands for Julia. "I'll just get this little lady ready for bed."

Kenneth looked at the clock. It was almost eight. "It is about time for little girls to be in bed." He leaned closer to Emma, and she heard her own intake of breath at his closeness. "It's been a busy day," he added, moving away.

She nodded her head. "Thank you for staying with me today. I don't know what I would have done without you."

He shifted in his seat. "I want to help. Can I get your pain pills for you?"

She shook her head. "I can do it." She looked at his face and the bruised eye he bore because he had come to her and Julia's rescue. She stood to softly touch his forehead just above the bruises. The tears slipped silently down her cheeks as she whispered, "I'll be grateful to you for the rest of my life."

She squeezed his hand and he squeezed back. His hands were warm in hers and her stomach fluttered a little at his touch. She pulled back, not sure what to do. She hadn't let anyone close to her since Paul, and these feelings were so strong, they scared her a little.

Kenneth smiled down at Emma, then took a deep breath. "You are exhausted and should be in bed. We've got a busy day tomorrow."

Pepper joined them as Kenneth helped Emma toward the stairs. "Julia's in the last room on the right. The bathroom is just down the hall, of course, and there's more clean towels on your bed."

"Thanks for everything. I loved hearing all those stories about Kenneth." She smiled slightly. "It was fun."

Kenneth glanced over his shoulder at Emma. "Yes, it was," he said quietly. He looked like he wanted to say more, but with a glance at Pepper it was easy to see he'd decided against it.

He turned back to Pepper and shook his finger at her. "You, however, are in trouble with your grandson for giving away all the family secrets."

Pepper laughed. "They're not secrets anymore, my boy. Half my ward has heard those stories."

Kenneth groaned. "Please tell me that's not true."

Emma smiled. "Good night." She put her hand on the banister. "You know you both are welcome at my table anytime, so I can return the favor." And with that she went upstairs.

Kenneth was quiet as he walked into the kitchen with Pepper.

"Penny for your thoughts," Pepper asked softly.

Kenneth looked at his grandmother incredulously. "As if I will ever trust you again, telling all my secrets like that." He draped his arm across her shoulders. "Especially the dog story. Please promise me you won't ever tell that story again."

She laughed so hard at his piteous expression, she could hardly grab the dishtowel from the oven rack.

Kenneth helped her finish drying the dinner dishes, feeling happy. All in all it had been a nice evening. He looked at Pepper wiping the tears from her eyes. It was good to be here. Even with all the craziness, he was glad he had come to Pepper's. His thoughts turned to Emma. He liked being needed by her. Somehow it made him feel a little better knowing she was safe tonight.

CHAPTER EIGHT

By eleven o'clock Emma knew she wouldn't be able to sleep. She lay rigid in her bed, hearing every noise and creak. She couldn't help it, she just didn't feel safe yet. She crept downstairs to the kitchen, opening the fridge for a midnight snack.

"Hello," Kenneth answered sleepily, from the doorway.

Emma jumped. "You scared me!" she exclaimed, her heart pounding.

"What's the matter, can't sleep?"

"Too many noises I'm not used to, I guess," she said, slightly embarrassed. "I thought maybe a snack would help."

Kenneth opened the fridge wider. "We could have another piece of pie," he suggested.

Emma knew she shouldn't, but couldn't resist. Key lime pie was her favorite. She brought out the pie and Kenneth flipped on the lights and got two plates and forks. He cut them generous slices and sat at the table. "So tell me about yourself."

Emma slowly took a bite, savoring the slightly sour taste. "Nothing to tell," she managed. "I'm a city attorney, I have a beautiful daughter, that's about it. Let's hear about you."

"I think Pepper took care of that, telling you all my embarrassing moments," he said wryly.

"Fill in the blanks for me," she asked.

"Well, I graduated from BYU with a degree in teaching, and I started teaching ninth grade English classes."

"When did you decide you wanted to become a lawyer then? The teenagers too much for you?"

Kenneth put down his fork. "My fiancée was wrongfully accused of fraud and embezzlement. She didn't have a good defense lawyer that actually cared whether she was innocent or not, and we were at his mercy. At first it looked like we were going to win the case, but the lawyer started to make mistakes and the case went south. My fiancée couldn't take it, and she killed herself."

Emma covered Kenneth's hand with hers. "Oh, Kenneth, I'm so sorry. That must have been horrible for you."

Kenneth shrugged. "After that I promised myself that no one would go through what Miriam did if I could help it, so I became a defense attorney and give the absolute best defense for my clients that I can. It's taught me a lot about not judging others until you have all the information."

"So how did you meet Paul?"

"I started at Carrington, Stone and James last year, and Paul was a partner there."

"No wonder you're so good with kids if you were a teacher." She took a bite, chewing carefully on the side of her face that wasn't as bruised. "So you never married then?" Emma asked, and blushed as soon as the words left her mouth.

Kenneth lifted one eyebrow. "No, haven't really had the time or inclination to date anyone seriously since Miriam."

"I bet the sports car gets you some hot dates."

"You might think that, but actually it doesn't. I'm not interested in those kinds of women. My grandpa and I always put together model cars when I was a boy. Then I grew up and wanted a real version of one, that's all."

Emma tucked that information away in her mind, and got up to pour them both a cup of milk. Reclaiming her seat, she cupped her drink, looking over at her companion. She really enjoyed being with him. Having Kenneth around had made her feel safe and she enjoyed their conversations. He was supportive and generous and she needed that. Her first impression that he was materialistic and cold had been so wrong.

"So did you go on a mission?" she asked as she carefully crossed her legs underneath her.

"I actually went to northern Alberta, Canada, so I can identify with your dad. It was a great mission. The people up there are like no other. They just seem to care about each other, and are very patriotic." He settled into his chair next to her. "The country is breathtaking. I've always wanted to go skiing there. The snow is just perfect for it."

"My dad and I always laugh at the stereotypical American idea that it's snowy there all year round. He was even asked once if he needed a driver's license to drive a dog sled."

He smiled. "No, the weather is practically the same as here. Summer is warm and sunny, spring is wet, but Canadian winters are definitely colder." He took a sip of his milk. "Is your dad Canadian?"

"Yeah. He's from Toronto," she said, then took a sip of her drink before asking, "Do you miss Canada?"

"Definitely. I've always intended to go back and visit the people there, but I never have."

"Why not?"

"I've been too busy building my career, I guess."

After an awkward pause, he changed the subject. "What are you thinking about this disk?"

"I'm not sure. If your firm was mixed up with Miera and Paul got in over his head . . ." She looked thoughtfully at the milk in her glass. "Paul was usually so wrapped up in himself, and I really didn't see any change in him after our divorce. But smuggling a disk out that shows possible money laundering, drugs, and bribery by a known terrorist . . . it's just so unbelievable."

"I didn't know him all that well, but he seemed like a very good lawyer."

"Oh, he was a good lawyer, that's for sure. He prided himself on that. Unfortunately that was his focus—being a good lawyer and making a lot of money. It didn't leave a lot of room for anything else."

Emma put down her cup, suddenly wanting Kenneth to know her past. "When we found out I was pregnant, Paul didn't want to keep the baby, but I did. I wanted a family. He made me choose, and we got divorced." She shrugged. "It was a tough time for me. He completely cut me out of his life. His parents didn't even know they had a granddaughter for months afterward. That hurt me for a long time and I was pretty bitter. But the missionaries found me, and becoming a member of the Church saved my sanity."

"That must have been very hard," Kenneth said, touching her hand. "You've done great as a single mother. Julia is a well-adjusted little girl."

Emma's eyes lit up. "She sure is, isn't she? Julia is worth everything to me. I would do anything for her. I love her so much." A shadow crossed her face. "I need to make sure she's safe. Maybe we should just go to a hotel until the police catch this guy."

Kenneth looked down, knowing it was a good idea, but not wanting their time together to end. He looked at his watch. "We'd better go to bed. I want to see if your father has replied to your e-mail first thing tomorrow. Are you sure you're up to this?"

She sighed. "I feel fine. Don't worry about me."

He pulled her up beside him, catching the scent of her hair.

It smelled good and he drew her a little closer. "I completely agree, counselor."

Emma let herself be held for a moment, then pulled away. "I better get to bed. Thanks for the pie and the conversation."

He reluctantly let her go and flipped off the lights. "You're welcome," he said as he watched her walk toward the stairs. "Glad I could help a fellow attorney in need. It's one of my specialties," he said to her back, a smile on his face.

She grinned, glancing over her shoulder at his expression. "Your grandmother was right about you. You do have a big head!"

Kenneth drew his eyebrows together. "She said that about me? I'm going to have a long talk with her!"

She laughed. "You're going to get me in trouble."

He caught up with her on the stairs and bent close. "I'll make it up to you," he said huskily, near her ear.

"I'll bet you think you can," she said staring straight ahead for a moment, not sure how to react. Her stomach was doing flip-flops. "We'd better go."

Kenneth nodded, then put his fingers to his mouth. "Shh, do you hear that?"

"What?" Emma said, her eyes large, the moment gone.

"I hear something scratching."

They went down the stairs. The noise seemed to be coming from the back door. Kenneth motioned for her to stay behind him. He jumped when someone jiggled the door handle on the other side.

"Go get the phone and call the police," he whispered to Emma. She stood motionless behind him, a look of fear on her face. Deep fear. He wrapped his arm around her and guided her back to the kitchen. He dialed 911 and quickly described the situation. Within moments they heard sirens.

Kenneth went to the back door, then came to the kitchen

where Emma was sitting at the table. "It looks like he's gone," he said.

She looked at him, but it was more like through him. Her eyes seemed dull and lifeless, the only emotion showing was fear.

Pepper came downstairs, still tying her robe around her. "What's going on?"

At that same moment a policeman knocked at the door. Kenneth checked through the peephole, then let him in.

They all went into the living room, Kenneth sitting close to Emma. She didn't know what to think. She felt frozen with fear, all the memories of the attack rushing back to her. She heard Kenneth talking to the policeman and wanted to speak, but couldn't.

The officer's partner came in and reported that there were fresh footprints in the snow, but he also had a small object in his hand. He held it out to Emma. "Recognize this?"

Emma nodded. It was her driver's license. "It was taped to the windshield of the sports car out there, and three of the tires were slashed."

"My driver's license was in my purse that was stolen two days ago," Emma managed to get out through her tears. "This guy is never going to leave me alone, is he?"

Kenneth hugged her tightly. "He will never get near you again, Emma, I promise."

Emma twisted gently away from his embrace. "You can't protect me, Kenneth. I think maybe I need to . . . oh, I don't know what to do," she moaned.

"I don't think you should make any decisions tonight," he said gently. "Is there any way you could bend some rules and put a policeman on the house until they catch this guy?" he asked the police officer.

"I'm sorry, but we really can't. I know this is frustrating.

I can put an extra patrol on the street, but right now that's all we can do."

Kenneth ran his fingers through his hair, making it look even more like he had just climbed out of bed. "I guess the good news is that you have your driver's license back."

Emma started to cry again. "This isn't funny."

He regretted his comments immediately. "I'm sorry, this is just so frustrating."

Julia came down the stairs and went flying into her mother's arms. "Why are the policemen here, mom?"

"It's okay, Julia," she soothed. "They're helping us." She looked over her daughter's head. It didn't look like anyone could protect them. What was next? Then it came to her. She needed to call her dad. She stood. "Pepper, can I use your phone?"

Emma spent the next two hours trying to track down her father. When she was finally patched through she nearly cried in relief. "Dad, it's me," she croaked out.

"What's wrong?" he immediately asked. "Why are you calling me? Didn't you get my e-mail?"

"No," Emma answered. "I haven't checked my e-mail yet."

"You need to get to the safehouse immediately, and take Julia," he said quickly. "I mean now! Take your coat and go, don't wait."

Emma looked over at Julia sitting with Pepper on the couch. "Why, what's going on?"

"I'm flying in to meet you there. Just hurry. I've got to go, sweetheart. I'll see you at the safehouse in two days," and with that the line went dead.

Emma went into the living room and took Julia's hand. "Come on, darling, we've got to go get dressed."

Pepper stood. "Where are you going at this time of night?"

"My dad is insisting on me leaving and going somewhere safe," Emma explained. "He's going to meet me there."

Kenneth stood immediately. "I'm going with you."

Putting her hand on his chest, Emma shook her head. "No, that's not possible."

"I'm not leaving you alone," he insisted.

Feeling tired, exhausted and emotional, Emma closed her eyes. "Okay, but we need to go now."

"You're not leaving me here alone," Pepper protested. "We'll all go." She shook her finger at Kenneth. "And I want to know exactly what's going on." Kenneth took her to her bedroom to help her gather a few of her things and filled her in briefly on what was happening and what they suspected. Pepper nodded and said, "It's best that we leave, just as Emma's father wants."

After gathering a few clothes, blankets and other items, the foursome piled into Pepper's car. "Where to?" Kenneth asked.

Emma directed him to I-15 and they headed north. Luckily the roads were dry and the traveling went smoothly. Julia fell asleep on her mother's lap in the backseat and Pepper had curled up on the passenger side and was snoring softly. Kenneth drove through the inky blackness, passing a few semi-trailers along the way but not much else. "Are you asleep, Emma?" Kenneth whispered.

"No," Emma replied. "I can't sleep in a car, or anywhere else that isn't my bed."

"That's never been a problem for me," Kenneth chuckled. "My parents always used to joke that I could sleep anywhere or through anything."

"Your family sounds wonderful."

"They are," Kenneth said warmly. "We were always so close. They never missed a basketball game I was in, or a band concert, they were there for me whatever it was. Even my sister."

"What's your sister like?"

"She has her moments, but I love her. She was always sort of my shadow since she was so much younger, and it bugged me then, but I'm glad she's around now. She just got married last year. What's your family like?"

Emma was quiet for a moment. "I don't remember much about my mother really, only soft images now. She died in a car accident when I was five. My father hired a nanny for me and threw himself into his job. He came home as often as he could, but I went months without seeing him." She smiled wistfully. "I met Paul and felt like I really belonged somewhere and to someone, and when that didn't work out I felt more alone than ever."

"What did you do?"

"Then I had Julia and it gave me the sense of family I'd always wanted. And when I met the missionaries and they took me to church for the first time, I found the sense of belonging I'd always dreamed of. The ward became the family I'd never had. It was really hard to move away from that to Utah. But I needed the money that being a city attorney offered me. I want Julia to have a good life."

"She has a good life. You are obviously a very good mother."

Emma shifted in her seat, trying to get comfortable without waking up her little girl. "Thanks. Do you ever think about having children?"

"Someday," Kenneth said softly, his thoughts focusing on the woman in the backseat. "When I find the right person." The more he learned about her the more he realized that she was not the fragile woman he first thought, but was strong and independent. He couldn't seem to get enough of her—to know the real Emma, to be part of her life. They came to a fork in the road and Emma directed him left. "Where are we going anyway?"

"To the Teton Valley in Idaho. We have a cabin there."

The brilliant light of the sunrise was just coming over the horizon and chasing away the purple night, glinting off the snow on the fields. Kenneth yawned. "Do you mind if I turn on the radio? I don't want to fall asleep at the wheel."

"I can drive for a while," Emma offered.

"No, it's okay, I like driving, I just need some music or something to help keep me awake." He flipped on the radio softly and found a station just finishing a song.

"And now for the news at the top of the hour," the announcer droned. "A large snowstorm is expected today and road conditions are expected to worsen as the day progresses. Utah police at this hour are looking for an Arizona attorney going by the name of Kenneth King for questioning in the death of a partner in his law firm. Anyone with information should call this number . . ."

Kenneth didn't hear anything else. The announcer's words echoed in his mind but he wasn't able to make sense of it. He was wanted for questioning in Paul's death! How could that be?

CHAPTER NINE

"Did he just say that you were wanted in Paul's death?" Emma exclaimed.

Kenneth nodded.

"What's going on?" she asked.

He shrugged. "I don't know, Emma. I honestly have no idea."

She rubbed her temples as if she had a headache. "Turn here," she instructed. "We need some gas."

They stopped at the little gas station and Kenneth got out to fill up. He clapped his hands together in the cold, anxiously waiting for the pump to finish. As soon as it clicked that it was done, he went inside to pay. Taking off his gloves, he looked around the candy aisle for a moment thinking a snack might help wake him up and noticed that one of the two cashiers was watching him closely. He smiled, but the other man didn't smile back. *Just get out of here*, the voice in his head urged.

He grabbed a newspaper and went to the counter, pulling his wallet from his back pocket and taking out some bills. The large cashier didn't seem to pay him any attention at all, but the small dark-haired one was still staring. Kenneth took his change, shoved it in his wallet and left. As he walked to the car, he looked back and could see the little man pointing at him while talking to the bigger man. Kenneth hurried and got in.

"I think that guy spotted me," he said as he put the car in gear and drove away. "How much further is this cabin?"

Emma looked out the back window. "The cabin is just ahead."

After a few more turns down a road that was getting smaller and smaller, Emma finally spotted the turn-off to the cabin. The small road had not been plowed in a while and the car slipped and slid up to a medium-sized log cabin. "Are we here?" Julia asked sleepily.

"We're here," Emma soothed. "I'll go and tuck you into bed, darling."

Kenneth helped the women out of the car, hefted Julia into his arms, and they waited while Emma unlocked the cabin door. She went inside, turning on the lights, and directed Kenneth to Julia's room. He put her down on the bed and Emma took off her shoes. "I'll go start the fire," Kenneth said.

Emma nodded, concentrating on getting her daughter comfortable in bed. After Julia was safely tucked in, Emma joined Kenneth and Pepper at the kitchen table. "I assume you told Pepper what we heard on the radio and the incident at the gas station?"

Kenneth nodded. "I didn't have anything to do with Paul's death. I want you to know that."

Pepper covered her grandson's hand. "This is all a mistake. Kenny could never hurt anyone." She looked at Emma's exhausted face. "You need to get yourself to bed. We'll talk about this when we've all had some sleep."

Kenneth agreed. "Do you need anything? Your pain pills, water, anything?"

"No, I know my way around here." She pointed to the other two doors. "There's one other bedroom and the other door is the bathroom," she said wearily.

"Pepper, you take the other bedroom, I'll take the couch in here," Kenneth said.

"Are you sure?" Pepper asked.

"Yes, let's get you two to bed."

Kenneth watched them go down the hall, then sat on the couch to remove his boots. He spread out the quilt Emma had gotten for him. His supposed involvement in Paul's death was obviously some sort of setup, but his first instinct was to turn himself in and get this taken care of, to clear his name, especially after being watched closely by that cashier.

However, remembering the look of fear on Emma's face at his grandmother's house changed his mind. He knew he couldn't leave them alone right now. "We'll just have to ride this out and hope Emma's father can help us," he murmured.

He watched the flickering flame in the fireplace for a moment, licking at the wood, crackling and popping as it devoured the log, and before long he was asleep.

&

When Emma emerged from her room she had dark circles under her eyes and didn't look like she'd slept at all. Kenneth was standing near the stove frying eggs, the tantalizing aroma of bacon surrounding him. "Good morning," he said and stepped to the pine table to pull out her chair for her. "How are you feeling this morning?" he asked.

Emma rotated her neck and took her seat near the bay window. "I didn't sleep much, let's put it that way. Where's Julia?"

"She's already eaten and is coloring by the fire with Pepper in the living room. She's pretty tired, too."

She looked out the window. "Looks like it snowed a little

bit." Kenneth put a plate in front of her, then sat down with the paper. "Where did you get that?" she asked.

"I grabbed it from the convenience store where we got gas."

He shuffled the paper for a moment and Emma ate in silence. "Any good news this morning?" she finally asked him. "Anything about your little, um, problem?"

Grimacing, he nodded. "It's on page 2. Not a lot of information really—just some details of Paul's death and my departure for vacation afterward. They say I'm a 'person of interest' and want to talk to me, but that's all. It does mention that I may be staying with a woman and her child." He closed the paper and slammed it on the table. "I know it's a setup because I was already questioned in relation to Paul's death. Besides, my mother knows where to reach me!" He took a deep breath. "That disk has been nothing but a nightmare for anyone who's had anything to do with it!"

At her look of surprise, he took her hand. "I'm so sorry I dragged you into this. If I'd just walked away from the Purple Turtle and left you alone, none of this would have happened."

Emma squeezed back. "I'm glad we're in this together," she said shyly. "It's been a long time since I felt like I could count on someone." She smiled and began eating again. "Besides if I knew you could cook, it might have changed my first impression about you."

"What was your first impression of me?" he asked, picking up the paper again.

"That you were a rich selfish lawyer," she said. "I was very wrong, and I want you to know that." They were silent for a moment, locking eyes, and something passed between them, an understanding. "Anything else interesting in the news today?" Emma asked, breaking the spell.

Kenneth blinked, as if surprised she had spoken. "There's a difficult case about a drunk driver that hit a busload of tourists on their way up to Sundance. Several of them had been seriously injured and one was killed." He turned the page to continue the article. "The drunk driver was not only driving on a suspended license for previous DUI offenses, he also had a blood alcohol of 0.18 at 10:00 a.m." The victims' cry for justice was appealing, but Kenneth knew as a lawyer that the drunk driver was still entitled to a fair trial. "It's probably going to be hard to get a fair trial with all this media coverage," he commented. "It could taint potential jurors."

Emma stiffened. "There shouldn't be any objectivity. He should go to prison for life."

"You know better than that. Everyone deserves their day in court."

"I just think the laws should protect us from people like that. How many lives does he have to destroy before he's put away?"

Her body language told Kenneth he'd better back off and fast. Her rigid back alone told him her nerves were taut. He quickly changed the subject. "So how's the food?"

Emma relaxed slightly. "Not bad. Where'd you learn how to cook?"

"Actually, that's one of the three dishes I know how to make well," he said sheepishly. "I work a lot and eat take out."

Emma glanced at him. "Then how do you keep your figure?"

"The law firm gave us a free pass to a local gym. I use it to get the stress out." He smiled. "So what are your plans for us today?"

"Just waiting for my dad, I guess. Why?"

"Is there a town nearby?" Kenneth asked. "I think we should go in for supplies and maybe see if there's more news about Paul's death or the investigation."

Emma frowned. "How can you even think about leaving here after the gas station? It's too dangerous. What if you're spotted? That would put us all in danger." She went to the long cupboard at the side of the sink and opened it. "Look, we have plenty of supplies. This cabin is very well-stocked."

"I could go alone. I can see how tired you are and I don't want you having a relapse on my account." He touched her chin briefly, putting the side of her face with the most bruises to the light.

Emma jerked her head away and looked at him sternly. "I'm fine. I just think we should wait for my dad, that's all. Why put ourselves in any danger when we're safe here?" She stood up and put her plate in the sink to rinse it off. "I brought some work to do. I have a case I'm working on that needs to be ready to go as soon as I get back."

"Can I help?"

"No," Emma responded automatically.

Kenneth shrugged. "Okay, but do you realize you just turned down the help of a very good criminal defense lawyer? I guess I'll just go into town."

Emma took a deep, exasperated breath. "Okay, you can help, if you promise you'll stay here."

Kenneth nodded as Emma continued. "And just so we're clear, I'm a city attorney, but a prosecutor at heart. I want to see our society rid of the people you defend so they can't hurt others. I'm not really sure if you can help me." She turned just as Pepper entered the room, overhearing her last sentence. Emma knew she was being abrupt, but somehow she couldn't help it. She just felt out of her element, out of control of her own life. She turned back to the counter to get hold of herself. "How did you sleep last night, Pepper?" she managed to ask.

Pepper stepped forward and hugged her, careful not to squeeze her shoulder and hurt her collarbone any further. "You look upset and exhausted. Why don't you go back to bed and when you wake up I promise that Kenny won't talk shop anymore."

Emma smiled wanly. "It's okay. I guess I still have some strong feelings about drunk drivers and defense attorneys."

Kenneth mentally kicked himself, remembering that Pepper had told him that Emma's mother was killed by a drunk driver. "I'm sorry if I upset you, Emma. It was unintentional. Why don't you rest today?"

"I really can't, but thanks anyway. I'll clean up a bit and then we can get to my case notes. I'll be ready in just a few minutes." She started down the hall and Kenneth followed her into the room she and Julia shared.

"Let me help you," he said, taking the blankets out of her arms and helping her make the bed.

"I can stand on my own two feet, you know," she chided.

"I'm sure you can," he said. "But I feel bad about bringing up drunk drivers when your mother . . ."

She put up her hand. "I don't want any pity. I'm a strong, capable woman. I'm a single mother with a daughter to think about, and if you think I need to lean on someone . . ."

Kenneth let the blankets fall to his feet and he took her face in his hands and gently kissed her, exploring her soft lips. It was one of the sweetest, most chaste kisses he had ever experienced. When he drew back, he said softly. "Emma, you don't have to tell me what kind of woman you are. I know every time I look at you."

She looked into his brown eyes, feeling swept away. "Kenneth, I . . ."

At that moment Pepper walked into the room, then froze. "Sorry, kids. I'll just come back later."

"No, Pepper, don't worry," Emma said with a smile. "A momentary lapse of judgment is all." She moved to the other side of the room, straightening the blankets.

Pepper glanced at Kenneth, his hands in his pockets, watching Emma finish the bed. "I'll keep Julia busy this morning," she said as she backed from the room.

"Thanks, Pepper," Emma called out.

Kenneth approached Emma and asked, "Do you want to talk about what just happened?"

"No."

"Emma, you can count on me, you know. You always come first with me. I feel like . . ."

She held up her hand. "Kenneth, as lawyers it's our instinct to analyze everything to death to try to see it from every angle. Let's not do that, okay?"

She moved past him to the door and then turned to face him. "I'm not sorry, you know, about letting my judgment slide and letting you kiss me." She looked into his eyes, wanting to read his feelings and thoughts.

He reached up to touch her cheek. "I'm not sorry for kissing you either. I've felt a connection to you from the first time we met. I am sorry that it's against your judgment, however. I mean to change that."

Their eyes locked, the tension thick between them. She felt his breath softly brushing her face. His admission of feeling connected to her felt right—she felt it too. But it was too soon. Wasn't it? After a moment she dropped her eyes and started for the door. "We've got work waiting for us. As soon as I'm showered and a little more awake, we can get working on it."

Kenneth trailed Emma to the bathroom door and left her to get ready while he joined his grandmother in cleaning up the breakfast. He didn't meet her eyes, but he was wearing a large smile. He'd told Emma how he felt about her and it had felt right.

Pepper didn't say anything, but just watched her grandson carefully. When the dishes were done, Kenneth leaned against the cupboard, watching the hall for Emma's appearance. "I think we should have a talk," Pepper said.

Kenneth was already on his way to the living room area. "Leave it alone, Pepper. I'm going to check on Julia and make sure the fire's still going."

He bent down to the massive fireplace made of rich stone. It was the biggest he'd ever seen. He poked the logs around, causing the flames to leap up again. He admired the huge pine mantle that hugged the muted gray stones. The fireplace was the centerpiece of the room with a stone bench running the length of it. It's warmth definitely permeated the entire cabin. He went over to the large picture window that took up most of the south wall next to the fireplace. "What are you looking at, Julia?" he asked.

The little girl had her face pressed firmly against the glass. "I thought I saw a bunny outside. I think he might want to come in."

"I don't think there would be any bunnies out there. It's too cold and they're probably warm and snug in their bunny houses for the winter."

"But what if he's lost and needs a place to stay?" she asked.

"I'm sure all the little bunnies are safe and sound in their houses," he reassured her. "Would you like me to tell you a story about bunnies? My sister Susan used to have a rabbit named Buster, and I could tell you about the time he got out and was chased by my dog."

Julia nodded and followed Kenneth over to the couch where she snuggled into his lap. He began his tale of the poor rabbit, while Emma quietly watched the exchange from the hallway. Her heart ached a little that her daughter hadn't had a father.

She hadn't experienced the earthly pleasures of having a dad around. She moved toward the living room, and was warmed by Kenneth's smile.

"Am I interrupting?" she asked.

Kenneth patted the seat next to him. "Not at all. Come and join us."

Emma sat down next to them and laughed at the story along with Julia. The three of them sitting there together felt warm and right to her. Before her thoughts could run away from her, she got up. "I'll go get my briefcase and we can get started."

Kenneth's arm felt bereft as she moved away from him. "No hurry," he said with a smile.

Emma settled her files on the kitchen table as Pepper poured hot chocolate for her and Julia, and they went into the living room. Kenneth also poured two cups of hot chocolate, then joined Emma. She pulled out a file and began to jot down some notes. Kenneth glanced over at it. "Ugh, I can't believe you're quoting Constitutional law cases. The research is so tedious."

She laughed at his grimace. "I love the ins and outs of it. Don't you find it awe-inspiring that everyone is entitled to rights guaranteed under the constitution?"

"Of course," Kenneth defended. "It's just not the most exciting thing I could think of."

"Do you really like being a criminal defense attorney? Don't you feel bad about helping people beat the system?"

He looked over his shoulder at Pepper helping Julia with her drink. "Now you're assuming they're all guilty. Not all my clients are criminals, you know."

Emma rested her pencil on the file. "But you can't be sure of everyone's innocence and yet you're compelled to defend them as if they were."

"A defense is a critical part of our justice system. Everyone is entitled to a good defense and if you didn't have defense lawyers, that wouldn't happen. Take what happened to Miriam. She was innocent, but her lawyer didn't believe in her or take the time to prove it." He leaned forward and looked at her earnestly, willing her to understand. "It helps me to give everyone the benefit of the doubt."

"But doesn't it affect you personally?"

He tapped his fingers on the table. "I've had some really tough cases to defend, and . . ." He creased his brow. "Of course it's tough. But I have to think that I'm vital to the justice system. And I'm good at what I do. I'm helping people. People like Miriam." He paused for a moment, then continued. "It definitely can be exciting. More exciting than constitutional law research."

Emma eyed him seriously. "I'm going for the opposite end of the spectrum. I don't care about excitement. I want to be a prosecutor that can help get the criminals off the streets." She shrugged. "Or a city attorney that can help a city put together an airtight legal and governing system that would keep law-abiding citizens safe."

He nodded. "A noble aspiration. It doesn't always happen, you know."

Emma looked down quickly, thinking of Paul. "Believe me, I know."

He touched her hand, and at his touch she tried to steady her own emotions. She smiled, then turned to look out the window, glad of the chance to hide her face in case her emotions would be easy to read. She breathed in, trying to get hold of herself. All of her feelings for a man had long-since been buried and it was disconcerting how strongly they were coming to the surface. There definitely was a connection between them.

She looked at him again, the strong jaw, the simple sincerity on his face endearing him to her. His morals and values seemed to be so easy for him to carry. As soon as the disk was taken care of perhaps they could explore these tender new feelings they were experiencing. It was exciting to her that she could keep up with him, verbally spar with him in the law arena, and still feel like she had his respect for her opinions, even if they were different than his own.

She settled back in her seat and began outlining the case to Kenneth and what she was trying to do. Kenneth made some suggestions to make her arguments stronger, arguing some of the issues represented. Emma had quoted several Supreme Court cases and she was interested in what he thought of her point of view. His quick mind played off of hers as they debated the issues back and forth. The adrenalin started pumping and she was really into the argument.

"It is not relevant to the case," she argued, passing him the papers. "The Supreme Court ruled on the merits."

He grabbed the paper from her, touching her fingers. "It could have been made relevant if it was argued properly," he shot back.

She drew back her hand, a thrill going through her at his touch. She looked up at him, realizing that he was waiting for a response to a question she hadn't heard.

"What did you say?" she asked.

He was saved from repeating the question when Pepper and Julia came in to show them the last masterpieces Julia had drawn. The adults oohed and aahed over them. "I think I'm going to put this little lady down for a nap," Pepper said.

Emma nodded. "Thanks for playing with her today."

Pepper shrugged. "I love having her around. She's my special girl, aren't you Julia?"

"Pepper, do you want to see my room?" Julia asked. "We could rest in there, couldn't we?"

Pepper smiled. "Of course, sweetie."

After Pepper and Julia left, the conversation lapsed. Both Kenneth and Emma were lost in their own thoughts. Kenneth finally gathered up the papers. "I think we're done with both of these, don't you?" Kenneth asked her.

Emma sat very still, not answering. She didn't look at him, just continued to stare out the window. He cupped her chin, turning her to face him. "Are you okay?" he asked.

"I'm fine," she said automatically.

"Be honest with me, Emma."

"I'm scared," she admitted.

She looked into his deep brown eyes and was sure he saw the deepest secrets of her heart. He bent his head and gently kissed her. "We'll get through this together," he promised. Kenneth took a deep breath, watching her. Her face was healing and her bruises had turned to a yellowish purple. But the bruises and injuries on the outside were nothing compared to her wounds on the inside, he knew. Every ounce of him wanted to protect her from further harm. "Would you consider seeing a counselor when all this is over?" he casually asked.

Emma shook her head slightly. "No, I can do this on my own."

Kenneth sighed. "Emma I deal with the criminal end of things, but I've seen enough victims to know that sometimes it helps to talk things through with someone. Think of Julia."

"I am thinking of Julia. She's the only thing keeping me together." Emma felt the tears begin to threaten again just looking at him and seeing his concern for her. One lone curl had escaped and fell onto his forehead. The bruise under his eye was yellowish now, but somehow it didn't look ugly to her. She knew exactly what she owed to Kenneth King for saving her and getting her through this ordeal.

Emma shook her head. "I can handle this. Really. But if it makes you feel better I will consider seeing someone when this is over."

"Okay, I'll let this go, but I'm going to say one more thing.

I understand you are a very independent woman and I admire that. But you don't have to prove anything to me. I just wanted you to know that," he said, allowing the subject to drop. He watched her for a moment. She was wearing a deep green sweater and her hair was pulled back in a ponytail, but some small tendrils had escaped and were hanging just past her ears, where small pearl earrings rested on the ear lobes. The small amount of makeup she applied accented her high cheekbones and creamy complexion. While the bruises had begun to fade and she'd been able to hide a lot of them, traces could still be seen. It reminded Kenneth how strong she was and gave her beauty an air of vulnerability.

"Why don't we get a snack, then we can go check on Pepper and Julia?" he suggested.

Emma nodded. "I think I should have rested with them."

"Well, we skipped lunch, too, which likely didn't help." He got up and went over the cupboards. "What about some soup?"

With the soup warming on the stove, they settled back at the table. Emma watched the snow glinting like diamonds, the trees standing guard over the treasure, dark and bare. It was a beautiful landscape. She put her head in her hands, feeling a headache coming on, the emotions of the last few days catching up with her.

"Penny for your thoughts," Kenneth said.

Sighing, she looked at the man seated next to her and instinctively knew she could trust him with her innermost thoughts. "I'm angry with Paul for putting our daughter in jeopardy," she said honestly. "He never cared about her from the beginning and he didn't care about her well-being when he told you to give me this disk. He must have known it would be dangerous." She paused and grabbed a napkin from the table as the tears started to fall. "Sometimes I feel so angry at him for not wanting her."

Kenneth didn't reply, taking her hand instead. He couldn't imagine anyone not wanting their own child, but then he wasn't Paul James. He just let Emma talk, glad she felt she could share this with him.

"At least I can be glad we're safe here," she continued. "You don't know how much I've appreciated having you and Pepper here with me."

Kenneth squeezed her hand. "Safety is our top priority."

Emma looked at him gratefully. "It feels good to have another adult to share things with. I've never really had that."

"I care about you, Emma, and I care about your daughter. I couldn't bear it if anything happened to either one of you, especially after I was the one that gave you the disk in the first place."

"It's not your fault. None of this is your fault, you must know that." She settled back in her seat as Kenneth got up to serve the soup. She started to stand to help him, but he waved her back. "I don't want you dropping this with your injured collarbone. Let me serve you."

They ate the soup, enjoying the comfortable silence. When they were both finished, Kenneth put the dishes in the sink and reached for Emma's hand. "Why don't you go rest and I'll clean things up here?"

"Well, I better go see where Pepper and Julia ended up so we know there is a free bed around here," she chuckled. "Pepper is very patient with Julia. She can be a handful."

She walked down the hall and opened the door to Pepper's room. It was empty. Going a little further, she opened her bedroom door. Pepper was sleeping soundly on the bed, but Julia was nowhere to be seen.

CHAPTER TEN

Emma walked to the large log pine bed and gently shook Pepper. "Pepper, where's Julia?"

"What do you mean?" Pepper said groggily, opening her eyes. "She's right here." Sitting up she saw the empty place beside her where Julia should have been. "She was right here."

Emma took a deep breath and started searching the house. "Julia, Julia," she called, looking under beds and in closets. Kenneth and Pepper also joined the search. It didn't take long to go through every nook and cranny and realize she wasn't inside of the cabin. They met in the kitchen. "How could she have gotten out without us seeing?" Emma said, short of breath. "We were here by the door the whole time."

"The window in the bedroom is unlocked," Pepper said. "I am so sorry, I should have been watching her closer. I just closed my eyes for a minute . . ."

"It's not your fault, Pepper," Emma said, giving the older woman a hug. "We're all tired."

Kenneth snapped his fingers. "She was talking earlier about seeing a bunny outside and thinking it needed to come in. Maybe she's gone after it."

Emma went to the coat hooks and took down her coat.

"I'm going to search for her."

"I'll go with you. Pepper, you should stay here in case she comes back."

Pepper nodded. "At least her coat was in the bedroom and she had the sense to put it on."

"She can't have gone far," Emma said, zipping up her coat, her hands shaking. "She's so little."

Kenneth took her by the arms. "We'll find her."

Opening the door, they searched the porch and the perimeter of the house. Small footprints could be seen all around the window near the fireplace. Then they disappeared into the trees.

Emma shot on ahead, but Kenneth grabbed her arm. "Let's say a prayer," he suggested.

Nodding, she pointed at Kenneth. "You say it, okay?"

After a short prayer asking for Heavenly Father's help in locating her, they continued their search. Picking their way through the snow they followed the footprints. The small hills looked as if someone had put a generous helping of whip cream on them. The air was cool and crisp, but the sun was shining. "It should be easy to spot her," Emma reasoned.

Kenneth nodded. He didn't want to scare Emma with his thoughts that maybe Julia hadn't wandered off by herself. He hoped that wasn't the case but with the events of the last few days it was a possibility. They started for the stand of trees, following the trail of tiny footprints. They zigzagged back and forth and then set out over the small rolling hills next to the cabin.

Emma tried to keep her face impassive and not show how scared she really was. She couldn't bear it if anything had happened to Julia, so she refused to think about that and quickened her pace. She crested the hill and groaned. More trees! She started down the slope, pushing the snow in front of her. Kenneth reached for her arm to steady her. "Whoa," he said.

"Slow down or we'll be rolling down this hill."

She smiled wanly and continued down. They started calling for Julia again, saying her name over and over until it echoed with Emma's heartbeat. Her legs were cold, her breath coming in short gasps, puffing in the air before her. But all she could think about was her little girl and how cold she must be. They had to find her!

Kenneth could see Emma's fright and did his best to calm her, but he was admittedly scared himself. He'd noticed adult footprints near the little girl's trail not too far back. He prayed it was just a coincidence.

Just then Emma grabbed his arm. There was a small red mound underneath a tree about a hundred yards ahead of them. Emma began to run, calling Julia's name. As they reached the little girl, Kenneth gently lifted her head. Her eyes were drowsy, but she responded. "Hi, Kenny."

"Hi, yourself, Julia." He began to lift her in his arms, but she reached for her mother.

"Mommy, I'm cold," she complained. "And I want to go to sleep."

Emma voice wavered as she tried to control her emotions. "Let Kenneth carry you home sweetheart and we'll get you warmed up."

Julia snuggled close to Kenneth and they started the long walk home. Emma had a hard time keeping up with Kenneth's long strides, but it was helping her own coldness dissipate. When they finally were in sight of the cabin they instinctively quickened their step. Kenneth had tried to keep Julia awake, knowing how dangerous hypothermia can be. She kept closing her eyes and complaining of how tired she was, but was able to answer all of his questions.

"I thought I saw the bunny and I was trying to help him get home," she told him. "I kept looking for him, but then I was cold and wanted to go in," her eyes closed again. "I was lost and tried to find the cabin again but I couldn't so I sat down and waited."

"Did you see anyone else?" Kenneth asked softly, out of Emma's earshot.

"No," Julia shook her head. "I said a prayer to Heavenly Father to keep me safe until you and mommy found me and he did," she said simply.

Kenneth hurried inside and found Pepper waiting at the kitchen table with hot chocolate. "Oh, you found her," she breathed with a sigh of relief.

"Hypothermia may be setting in," he said, taking her into the living room and setting her on the couch.

Pepper jumped into action, her nursing skills never forgotten. "The first thing we need to do is get her warm." She got a bowl and began to fill it with lukewarm water. "Go to the linen closet and get towels Emma," she instructed. She took off Julia's boots and socks, putting her feet into the bowl.

Julia moaned. "It hurts, Pepper."

"I know it does sweetheart, but we need to get you warm," she said firmly. "Kenny, get a fire going." She took off Julia's coat and took the towels from Emma. "Get her some warm pajamas," she didn't mince words. Rubbing Julia's feet with the towels to dry them, she then turned to Julia's hands and repeated the same procedure. "Kenny, get some hot soup going so we can warm her from the inside."

When Julia was settled in warm pajamas before the fire, Emma sat down to help her drink her soup. She couldn't even explain how relieved she was that Julia was safe and that Pepper had been here to help her. Emma wouldn't have had the first clue on how to treat Julia. She was a very lucky little girl. Pepper didn't think there would be any permanent damage.

She hugged Julia close to her. She was safe, her heart wanted to shout, but instead humbly thanked her Heavenly Father.

"We'll have to watch her closely during the night," Pepper said. "Do you want me to stay up with her?"

"No," Emma refused. "I want to be near her. Why don't you go to bed, Pepper? It's been a long day. Kenneth, you could take my bed and I'll stay out here by the fire with Julia."

Kenneth shook his head. "I'll stay up with you a while longer."

"Well I'm going to bed then," Pepper said. "Call me if you need me," she instructed. "See you in the morning."

Kenneth bent down to kiss Julia on the top of her head. "Good night, little lady," he said softly.

"Kiss Mommy, too, Kenny," she said sleepily.

Kenneth was startled at the request. He bent down, and Emma's face froze. *Am I really going to kiss her with Julia right here?* he wondered, remembering the kiss from earlier that day and Emma's reaction to Pepper seeing them together. Instead, he brushed his lips across her forehead and looked in her eyes as he drew back. He wanted to smile at the little look of disappointment he saw in her eyes. His own reaction told him he was starting to have very strong feelings for her. Emma shivered, and he didn't think she was cold.

He went around the cabin, checking all the doors and windows to make sure they were locked. Kenneth watched out the large picture window for a moment, noticing that a light snow was beginning to fall. He thought about his afternoon with Emma, savoring the sweet smell of her hair and the softness of her skin, and how grateful he was they were able to find Julia safe and sound. He settled next to Emma on the couch. Julia was finally sound asleep in her arms. "It seems a shame we have to wake her to make sure she's all right."

Emma hugged her daughter tighter. "I don't care as long as

she's here safe beside me. That was too close of a call for me."

He slid his arm around Emma. "I'm glad we found her safe. Did you hear her say how she'd prayed to Heavenly Father that we'd find her and she'd be safe?"

Emma shook her head. "I believe it, though. She's always been a very spiritual girl. She loves to go to Primary every week." She stroked Julia's hair. "I wish we could turn things back the way they were. Normal. Safe."

"Me, too. I wish we'd met under different circumstances, but . . ."

"I'm glad we met, too," Emma finished for him. She leaned back into his arms. They stayed like that, the three of them, watching the fire crackle, before falling asleep.

CHAPTER ELEVEN

Kenneth was instantly awake, his senses alerted to something. He realized they had fallen asleep with Emma's head on his chest, and she was still cradling Julia. He tried to shift their weight onto the couch, and as he did so he heard the noise again. It was a key jingling in the lock! He crept to the door, just as the key turned.

The door began to open and Kenneth waited behind it. As the shadowy figure stepped through the doorway, Kenneth tackled him to the floor, holding his hands behind his back. The man struggled, trying to release Kenneth's grip on him, shouting, "Get off me!"

The lights went on and Emma stood there. "Kenneth, let him go," she said loudly. "It's my dad!"

Her words registered in Kenneth's adrenaline-pumped mind and he released his prisoner. Helping him up, he extended his hand. "Sorry," he said sheepishly.

Emma's father did not return the handshake. "Who are you?" he demanded, turning off the lights and making sure the blinds were drawn tight. He went immediately to the far cupboard and pulled out a flashlight, making it clear he'd been here before and knew his way around.

"This is Kenneth King." Emma stepped forward into the small beam of light and hugged him. "It's a long story, Dad."

"What's going on?" Pepper appeared at the doorway, reaching for the lights.

"Leave them off," Emma's father barked and turned incredulously to his daughter. "And who is this?" he said to Emma, pointing at Pepper. "What did you do, bring your neighborhood?"

"Let's sit down, Dad," she said, motioning to the kitchen chairs. She placed a drowsy Julia on the couch and turned on a small lamp. She took her father's arm, and he winced in pain. Emma noticed blood on his shirt. "What happened?" she asked, helping him into a chair.

"It's just a scratch," he said, waving her away. "I just need the first aid kit from the bathroom."

"I'll get it," Pepper offered.

Kenneth stood near the door still observing Emma's father. He was about as tall as Kenneth, his dark hair streaked with gray. His face was rounder than Emma's, but they had the same brown eyes. His face was almost white, and Kenneth wondered how bad his wound really was.

Pepper came back with the first aid kit and knelt before the wounded man. "Let's take a look at this," she said. She began to tear his shirt just below the shoulder.

"I think introductions are in order if you're going to tear my clothes like that," he joked. "I'm Andrew Blythe, Emma's father. And you are?"

"I'm Penelope Davis, Emma's friend," she said mildly as she worked to clean the wound. "Would you like to tell us how you got a gunshot wound?"

He winced as she cleaned deeper. "They know you're here. I had to break through the lines they have surrounding you to get here. They're going to be moving in at daylight and I knew I needed to get to you now. I thought I had a clear run for it, but one of the guards spotted me and got off a lucky shot."

"You were lucky," Pepper pronounced. "It went clean through." She began to bandage his arm.

"Oh, Dad," Emma breathed. "We've got to get out of here."

Andrew caught his daughter's eye. "Yes, we do. I have an escape plan for you, me, and Julia. I didn't expect to have complications."

Emma looked away. "I needed them, Dad. They helped me after I was attacked, when Julia was lost..." she trailed off. "I needed them," she repeated.

"Well, I'm here now," he said. "You need to get packed because we're leaving within the hour."

"Where are you taking them?" Kenneth asked.

Andrew turned to face him. "Are you the man who gave my daughter that disk?"

"Yes, I did, on the request of Paul James," he said, wincing a little at her father's harsh tone.

He snorted. "Paul James never cared for the well-being of my daughter and he never deserved her or Julia. And for you to give that disk to my daughter was just short of stupid on your part."

"Dad," Emma gasped. "Kenneth had no idea . . ."

Her father cut her off. "I have no time for excuses. Now go get ready."

Emma stood her ground. "Not until you understand what's going on here. Kenneth and Pepper have been taking care of us. I never would have even gotten here if it weren't for them."

Andrew turned to face Kenneth and Pepper, his face serious. "Thank you for helping my daughter. She is in very capable hands now. I suggest you leave as soon as possible, since Miera's men know who you are and won't hesitate to kill anyone who gets in their way."

"Can't they come with us?" Emma asked. "They've risked their lives for me."

"I'm grateful for that, and if I'd known they were here I would have made arrangements for them," he said softly. Andrew gingerly stood to face his daughter. "Honey, there's a helicopter waiting that can only take two adults and one child. I need to get you out of here." He took her arms. "If you only knew how dangerous this is."

Emma folded her arms. "Why don't you tell me?"

Sighing, he looked down at his daughter's face and began. "I've been investigating Juan Carlos Miera for over fifteen years. He came onto the terrorist scene out of nowhere, joining up with the Martyr's Brigade first out of Colombia, then expanding into Argentina. No one has a picture of this man and he's able to slip easily through law enforcement's grasp, which means he's got a lot of friends in high places."

He raised his arm to run his fingers through his hair, then grimaced, remembering his injury. "He is ruthless and has well-documented ties to narcotics traffickers, mob bosses, money laundering, you name it, extending all the way to Canada. He found a cause in the Martyr's Brigade in fighting against the democracy and freedom that America and Canada enjoy, spreading hate to anyone who will listen. He engages in various sorts of attacks, including bombings of embassies and won't hesitate to murder, kidnap, extort and hijack anyone who gets in his way." He stopped and sat down again. "A month ago the chatter on the terrorist networks was that something big was coming. We got it narrowed down to Miera and his men, and that the attack was going to be in the United States somewhere, but we still didn't know when or where."

"Did the disk give you that information?" Emma asked.

Andrew nodded. "It did. It even gave us his itinerary. Do you remember seeing 'Peterson AFB, Colorado' on there?"

When Emma shook her head, he said, "NORAD is based on Peterson Air Force Base in Colorado Springs, Colorado."

"Why would the Canadians care about that?" Kenneth asked.

"NORAD is a partnership between the Canadians and Americans in protecting domestic airspace. They enforce the control of the skies over the United States and Canada." He looked over at Kenneth to see if he understood. "In 1989 during the invasion of Panama, the United States 'lost' a F-15 fighter jet with a GBU-15 still on it."

At Kenneth's confused look, Andrew explained further. "A GBU is a Guided Bomb Unit. It packs quite a wallop. Anyway, the U.S. kept it quiet, trying to locate it, but it was never found. Last year it miraculously found its way into the hands of Miera on the black market. An informant told us Miera was saving the bomb for something special, so both the Canadian and American governments were watching the Martyr's Brigade very carefully. When we got your disk, we knew what he'd been saving it for."

"So you think he's going to bomb NORAD?" Kenneth asked.

Andrew nodded. "Yes. Think about the message such an action would send to the world if our Aerospace Defense Command was bombed, eh? Our credibility in defending ourselves would be shot." He touched Emma's shoulder. "We've only got two days. I informed the American government immediately and everyone is on high alert. We're trying to keep it quiet though, so Miera doesn't know we're on to him. But my top priority is your safety. He knows you've seen the disk and he'll stop at nothing to get to you."

Kenneth sank down into the chair across from Andrew.

"That disk links a terrorist to my law firm."

Andrew nodded. "Your boss is Miera's brother. His real name is Eduardo. He and Juan Carlos had a falling out about five years ago and Eduardo came to the U.S. to start over with the law firm. Juan Carlos pulled him back into the fold by helping Vicente DiChesney, a drug kingpin friend of his, get out of any charges brought against him."

He sighed, then added, "Edward didn't really want to participate at first, but his brother convinced him that it was in his best interests. When he saw all the money coming in, Edward didn't protest too much after that."

"Why didn't the government close him down?" Kenneth asked incredulously.

"They haven't had any airtight evidence against him until now." He shrugged. "That disk provided names, dates, amounts—everything we've needed to see the inside of the network. The Green Credit Service and the Northwest Bank were the fronts for the money laundering operation, and the disk shows that your firm had several judges on the take. It was the missing puzzle piece."

"My fiancée once worked at Northwest Bank," Kenneth murmured.

Andrew wasn't listening. He pointed at Kenneth. "Edward figured out that Paul had given the disk to you. He traced you to Emma when he realized you'd gone to Utah for a vacation and Paul had an ex-wife in Utah. As far as I know, they don't know my connection with Emma or that you've given the disk to anyone else. They're desperate to get either the disk back or the two of you killed. I . . ." He held up his hand. "Do you smell that?"

"Smoke," Emma breathed.

Pepper took a few steps down the hall. "There's smoke billowing out of the back bedroom!"

Her father immediately went into action. "Where's Julia? We're leaving."

"She's in the living room." She grabbed their coats off the hooks. "I'll get her."

Pepper and Kenneth followed trying to shove on their boots and coats. "Should we drive the car?"

"No, they'll have that covered," Andrew shot back. "The best we can do is a motorcycle outside the passage." He talked as he walked toward the living room.

"What's the passage?" Kenneth asked, hearing cars outside and feeling the urgency of their escape.

"I don't have time for this," was all he said. "Just follow me."

Emma bundled Julia up as best she could, the smoke billowing in fast now, flames easily seen in the hall. She stood before the fireplace with her father. "Okay, I'm ready."

Andrew ran his hand along the stone exterior of the fireplace and gently pushed on a small indentation. The panel drew back revealing a stone staircase. He shined his flashlight into the opening then started down, reaching back for Emma.

Kenneth took his grandmother's arm. "Let's go," he said, helping her to the stairs.

They felt their way down the stairs which leveled off into a passageway. It seemed to go on forever. The dampness permeated Kenneth immediately and he was glad Emma had wrapped Julia in a blanket as well. The foursome walked along in silence, although Kenneth took Julia out of Emma's arms, concerned about her broken collarbone. "Thank you," Emma whispered, earning a stern look from her father.

"Let's move," he said. "We've got to make the rendezvous before daylight."

After walking for more than an hour, they saw a light at the end of the tunnel. The ladies were tired and seeing the light helped them renew their energy. As they approached the entrance they stepped around a small motorcycle, then toward the daylight, with Andrew leading them slowly toward it. He took a small radio out of his coat pocket and said something into it quietly. Within minutes a helicopter came into view.

Julia was wide awake and very excited about seeing a helicopter so close. "Look Kenny, here it comes," she said.

"Shhh," her grandfather said.

Julia's face fell. "Why is he so cranky?"

Kenneth shrugged. "I think he's worried about you and your mom, that's all," he soothed.

Emma joined them, tucking the blanket around Julia again. "We're going to get to go on the helicopter. Won't that be fun?" she whispered.

Andrew came up to the little group. "Okay, it'll be landing in a few seconds. We'll have you, Julia and your friend here," he jabbed a finger at Pepper, "get on the helicopter. They'll drop you off in Jackson Hole where my friend is meeting us."

"What about you and Kenneth?" Emma asked.

"We'll take the motorbike and meet you there," he said simply.

Emma looked doubtfully at the bike. "That's not big enough for the two of you. Kenneth and I should go. Besides, you're injured."

Her father immediately shook his head. "You're going and there's no argument."

The whoosh of wind signaled that the helicopter had landed. Andrew bent low, pushing Pepper and Emma in front of him. When Pepper was safely loaded on, Andrew took Julia and handed her to Pepper. He turned to help Emma up, but gunfire rang out, hitting the metal blades of the helicopter and making sparks fly.

Emma jumped back and stumbled toward the tunnel opening

as more gunshots ricocheted around her. Kenneth met her the last ten steps, trying to shield her as she fell into his arms. They watched for a moment as the helicopter safely took off with Pepper, Julia, and Andrew inside.

"Let's get this motorbike started," Kenneth said. "They've probably figured out where we are by now."

"Do you know how to ride one of these?" Emma asked.

"I guess we'll find out," Kenneth said as he grabbed the key that was magnetized to the bike. He got it started, then he snapped on his helmet and handed the other one to her. "Get on."

Kenneth gauged the road ahead of them, thankful it looked like it had been plowed and treated with gravel, but wishing that he was more experienced on a bike. He'd ridden for a summer before his mission but that was about it. *Let's hope it all comes back to me quickly,* he thought. When Emma's arms were securely around his waist, he revved the engine one more time, then took off as fast as he dared through the opening. Gunfire immediately assailed them, but the couple ducked low and kept going.

As soon as they cleared the trees Kenneth could see two SUVs following them. He didn't dare go any faster because of the road conditions, and he hoped that somehow they could outrun the larger vehicles. Emma's arms squeezed tightly around him and he knew she was frightened.

A fork in the road was just ahead of them and Kenneth took the left turn, hoping it would lead them to Jackson Hole. Just as he crested a small hill, the helicopter buzzed behind them to slow down the SUVs.

They backed off a little, but then Kenneth heard gunfire. Realizing they were shooting at the helicopter and not at them, he focused on the road and staying upright. Grateful for the helicopter's support, he said a prayer in his heart that they would get through this. The helicopter came in for another buzz just as one SUV closed in on the motorcycle. Kenneth lurched the bike to the right, and as he struggled to stay on the road, he saw Andrew lean out of the helicopter and shoot at the SUVs. He hit the first one several times, and it rolled to a stop. Smoke billowed from the engine, and two men jumped out, waiting for the trailing SUV to pick them up.

Kenneth used the reprieve to pick up the pace. A small road sign said Jackson Hole was fifteen miles ahead. *Fifteen miles! How will we ever make it?* he thought. He felt the presence of the helicopter overhead and was glad that Pepper and Julia were safely in the air.

Within moments the SUV closed in again, shooting at the helicopter. The helicopter backed off immediately and the SUV took the advantage to speed ahead. The SUV's front bumper slammed into the bike's back tire, sending the bike into a slide. He felt Emma's arms tighten around him as the edge of the canyon loomed toward them. As they went over the edge, the pair flew free of the bike and tumbled down the hill.

Emma quickly came to rest against a tree, but Kenneth careened headfirst through a patch of boulders. If he hadn't worn his helmet, death would have been instantaneous. *Heavenly Father, please watch over us,* he prayed before losing consciousness.

CHAPTER TWELVE

Kenneth heard the drone of a plane engine. He tried to sit up, but the pain in his head was too much and he sank back down.

"Thank goodness you're awake," Emma whispered. "I was so worried about you." He realized his head was resting on Emma's lap.

"Where are we?" he asked.

"On a plane. We've been captured."

He tried to sit up again, succeeding in coming to a semi-sitting position, but as soon as he put his wrist down, white hot pain shot through it. He held it and leaned back against some boxes behind him. "I think my wrist might be broken."

"Shh, don't talk, just rest." Emma brushed a curl away from his face.

"Are you okay?" he asked.

"I'm fine except for a few cuts and bruises," she replied. "Just walking away from that crash alive is a miracle." Her voice broke. "You were unconscious for so long. I didn't know what to do. I couldn't bear it if anything happened to you." She gently squeezed his arm, the emotion apparent.

He smiled, but it looked more like a grimace. "It's okay, I'm fine, just a little headache and a hurt wrist." He shifted so he could put his arm around her. "Shh, don't worry, we're going to be fine."

She allowed herself to be held for a moment, then drew back and pulled his handkerchief from her pocket. "How do you know that? We're in a plane with men who want to kill us." She started to dab at blood that had trickled down his face.

Kenneth winced and glanced over at the pilots. He met the eyes of the co-pilot, who watched him for a moment, then flicked his glance to Emma. His look was pure evil and it sent chills down Kenneth's back. His every instinct was to put Emma behind him and stand between them. He was glad her back was to the co-pilot and she couldn't see his stare. "You know this is the first vacation I've taken in three years and I never thought I would spend it this way," he said, keeping his tone light as the co-pilot turned back to the controls.

Emma couldn't help but laugh. "Is that all you can think about?"

"It was worth it to see you smile," he said, lightly squeezing her shoulder. He watched as she took off her scarf and made a makeshift sling out of it, tying it behind his neck. She was so close he could feel her breath on his cheek. Leaning closer he touched his lips to hers. She reciprocated, combing her fingers through his hair and drawing him closer. As the kiss deepened it was as if their souls were meeting again after a long absence, their breath mingling, sharing and reciprocating, making all else fade away.

Emma was the first to draw back. "You should rest," she said breathlessly, touching his cheek.

He nodded, not sure of his voice. He looked over at the pilots again, but neither of them was paying attention to their passengers. Kenneth and Emma settled back against the boxes covered with heavy netting, not able to see much as darkness approached. "They've certainly given us first class accommodations," he grimaced. "Tell me what happened after we crashed," he asked, drawing her close with his good arm. "Did they say where we were going?"

"I overheard one of them say we're going to Colorado Springs, but that's all I know. They dragged us up the hill after the crash and drove us to the airport in the SUV. They weren't very gentle with you, I'm afraid." She tucked her hair behind her ear. "Before I knew it we were being loaded on this plane." She shuddered. "They told me if I tried to escape, they'd kill me. I believe they would have, too."

"You did the right thing to obey them. We're alive and we're together. We'll get through this."

The pain in Kenneth's wrist was subsiding somewhat, but the pain in his head was making him dizzy. He closed his eyes and dozed off. After what seemed like just a few minutes, Emma was shaking him awake. "We're landing."

"Are we in Colorado Springs?" he asked groggily, trying to clear his mind of the fog.

"I think so," she said. "Are you all right?"

"I'm a little dizzy, that's all," he assured her.

Just then the co-pilot came toward them, jerking Emma's arm as he drew her to a standing position. "Hey, you're hurting me," she cried.

Kenneth got up quickly, but his dizziness assaulted him and he stumbled toward them. "Leave her alone," he called out.

The small man just sneered. "What are you going to do about it?" He pulled Emma against him and showed Kenneth the gun he held in his other hand.

"Kenneth, don't. It's okay," Emma said, her eyes pleading.

"Follow me," the man with the gun ordered, forcing Emma to walk with him. Kenneth acquiesced and followed the pair to the door, desperately trying to clear his head of the dizziness.

A large man climbed the airplane's steps and joined them, a gun slung low over his shoulder. "These are the two who have caused all the problems?" he asked, and the small man nodded.

"Let's get them inside quickly." He then turned to Kenneth and said, "And don't even think about doing something stupid."

Kenneth just stared at them, trying not to give away how badly he felt. His wrist and his head were both throbbing now. The large man pushed him toward the door, making him stumble. "Hurry up," the man growled.

"Hey, you don't need to do that," Emma lashed out. "Can't you see he's hurt?"

"Shut up," the smaller man told her, jerking her toward him. "Just do what you're told."

Emma pushed away from him. "There's no need for violence."

He took her arm and twisted it. "Americans don't know of any way to solve problems other than violence." He pointed the gun at Kenneth. "Get moving."

"What do you mean, we're a peace-loving people." Emma carried on the conversation as she took in her surroundings. They were at an airstrip, with two small hangars. The plane had landed about fifty feet from the largest one and that's where they were heading.

"Peace-loving," he snorted. "You invade other countries and overthrow governments, all under the name of *peace*. You disgust me."

"Well, you look like an American to me," she countered. "If you're not American, where are you from?"

"You are about to be a part of history. This is the day that

Americans will know that the world will no longer stand for
their sinful ways. We will show the world that there are people
willing to stand up to America and that America is not as strong
as she appears." He laughed, slapping his gun.

Another man came toward them on the tarmac. Kenneth
immediately recognized him as Chad, the security guard from
the law firm's parking garage. "Tony, are you still yapping?
We've got to get them to the rear office. The boss will be here
any minute."

Chad eyed Kenneth and slowly raised an eyebrow as if daring
him to say something. His tall thin frame was a sharp contrast
to Tony's large muscular one, but it was obvious who was in
charge.

"Don, let the girl go," Chad said, and the small man promptly
did so. Chad looked at Emma. "Did you have a nice trip?"

"Do you really care?"

"Not really," he said nonchalantly and turned away.

Emma was finally allowed to join Kenneth as the group
walked toward the hangar. Emma helped Kenneth as much
as she could, grateful for his presence. When they reached the
hangar, they walked past the large warehouse area into a back
door which seemed to lead to offices. They walked down a
small hallway which was lined with doors and then forked off
down another hallway lined with doors. Their footsteps echoed
on the concrete floor, and everything had an eerie glow from
the fluorescent lighting. Kenneth and Emma were led to the end
of a hall and were pushed inside a room. Tony locked the door
behind them. "That'll keep 'em until the boss gets here," Emma
heard him say.

She helped Kenneth to the small couch in the office and he
sank down heavily. "I can't shake this dizzy feeling," he said.

"I know," she soothed. "You probably have a concussion.

Just try to rest." She sat down next to him. "We've got to think of a way out of here so we can warn someone."

Kenneth opened his eyes. "Under no circumstances are you to do anything. I don't want you getting hurt."

Emma stood up. "Last I checked you weren't my father." She bent down to look at the lock on the door and jiggled the handle. "It's definitely locked." She started going through the desk drawers which were empty. "Not even a paper clip," she announced, disgusted, and sat back down next to Kenneth. He put his arm around her.

"Just stay here with me," he asked. "I want you safe."

Emma seemed not to hear him. "If I could just get to the office two doors down. I saw a phone and a computer in there. I could contact my father and tell him where we are." She looked up at the heating duct.

"Don't even think about it," Kenneth warned. "You're small, but you're not *that* small."

Emma punched his arm. "Hey, you better be nice."

A moment later they both sat up when they heard footsteps coming down the hall. A key jiggled in the lock and Tony stood before them. "Come on, let's go," he said gruffly. "The boss wants to see you." Tony turned around to lead the way.

"Create a diversion," Emma whispered in Kenneth's ear. He looked down and she'd taken off her shoes. His arm tightened around her.

"No," he whispered back. But before he knew it she had ducked out of his arm and was down the hall and softly closing a door into another office.

Kenneth briefly closed his eyes, knowing he couldn't attack Tony in the condition he was in, so he just kept walking, praying Emma was safe and could get through to someone on the phone. They'd only taken about fifteen steps when Tony turned to look at them.

"Where's the girl?" he shouted, reaching for his gun.

Kenneth stayed silent, and Tony started back down the hall. "She'll be sorry when I find her."

Kenneth took a gamble, ramming into Tony with all his might, sending Tony flying forward. "Emma," he called out frantically. "They know you're gone."

Tony scrambled to his feet and stuck his gun in Kenneth's face. "I wish I could blow your head off," he said. "Maybe later."

Tony then motioned Kenneth back down the hall and into another office, but this one was lavishly decorated. "I need to find your girlfriend, but I promise I'll kill you if you try anything else."

Kenneth stood in the middle of the office for a moment, trying to get his bearings. There was a bookcase on one end, and a large desk in the middle. Several computers lined one wall and there was a small refrigerator and microwave to the side of the computer table. Leather wingback chairs were set strategically throughout the room.

He walked to the window and watched as a fighter jet landed next to the other hangar. A man emerged from the plane, walked into the hangar and then disappeared from sight. Kenneth nervously waited a few more minutes, praying that Emma had found a way to contact her father.

Kenneth's hope for a safe resolution quickly faded, though, as the door opened and Edward Carrington walked through it.

CHAPTER THIRTEEN

Edward Carrington stood in the doorway for a moment watching Kenneth, then walked slowly behind the desk. "I'm sorry to keep you waiting, Kenneth. Your friend seems to have escaped us momentarily."

Kenneth tried to calm his frayed nerves. "What's this all about, Mr. Carrington?"

Carrington drew the blinds over the window, shielding them from the last rays of the sunset. "I think you know what this is about. Where is the disk?"

"It's in a safe place," Kenneth said, his stomach tightening.

"Have you looked at it?"

"Yes, but it was encrypted so I couldn't read it. I was very surprised that Paul would give me a disk I couldn't read."

"Paul was a fool," Carrington muttered under his breath. "He betrayed this firm, and don't think I'm not aware of what you've been doing these past few days." He pointed a finger at Kenneth. "You're as bad as Paul. No loyalty at all."

Kenneth tried to steady his voice. "What do you mean?"

Before Carrington had a chance to answer, the door opened and a large man strode toward Kenneth, immediately shoving him toward the wall and patting him down. "Hey," he protested.

A uniformed man filled the doorway, slowly entering the room. "I apologize for the way Jorge is treating you, Mr. King, but I must make sure you didn't bring any unauthorized items," the man said. He then turned to Carrington. "Good to see you again, Eduardo."

Carrington looked surprised to see the newest visitor. "John, why are you here? Didn't you think I could handle it?"

"Eduardo, this is the biggest operation the Martyr's Brigade has ever had. Did you really think I would entrust it to anyone but myself?"

"Don't call me Eduardo,'" Carrington said, his voice rising. "We are in America. Call me Edward."

"Little brother," Juan Miera laughed. "Does it really matter? America will be brought to her knees in less than two hours. You will not be so sensitive then."

"Any sign of the disk, Eduardo?" Miera asked, picking imaginary lint off his immaculate general's uniform.

At Carrington's shake of the head, Miera signaled to Jorge, who slammed Kenneth into a chair and tied his hands behind his back. Kenneth felt as if his injured wrist was going to explode. Jorge searched him again, this time removing Kenneth's left shoe and finding it there. Kenneth felt disappointment sweep through him, as Miera grabbed the disk from Jorge.

"Please just let me go now," Kenneth said. "You've got what you want."

Miera cracked a smile. "Do you really think we're going to let you walk out of here?"

Carrington held up his hand. "Kenneth, I always thought you were a promising attorney. Do you like it better than being an English teacher?"

He seemed sincere, but Kenneth didn't buy it. Instead, he just stared at Carrington, who said, "No answer? It might surprise you to know we've watched you closely for the last five years, bugged your phones, and tracked your movements. I don't think you ever suspected a thing."

"Why would you bother tracking me?" Kenneth asked.

Carrington gave a smirk. "We started to expand the 'business' to the bank where your fiancée worked. What was her name again?"

Kenneth didn't answer, his mind racing.

Carrington shrugged. "No matter. The bank president was easy, he had a history of bad gambling debts and had been cooking the books for years. When your fiancée started nosing where she didn't belong, she found us out and she had to be taken care of."

"What are you saying?" Kenneth asked.

"I think you know," Carrington replied. "She hired that moronic attorney, so we thought she would lose easily, but he started winning. So we bought him off, along with the judge. Of course, we had to kill her to be safe."

Kenneth listened in horror as Carrington continued, "We made it look like a suicide, and the investigation was closed quickly. Our only question was whether she ever told you what she knew."

Kenneth struggled against the ropes binding him to the chair. "You killed her!" he said incredulously, his face contorted with pain and anger.

Edward sat down on the edge of the desk, unperturbed by Kenneth's actions. "We were convinced that she had told you, since you suddenly changed careers and jumped at the chance to work for my law firm. We knew we either had to bring you in—or take you out."

Kenneth eyed the men, his jaw set, the shock still apparent on his face. "But why did you have to kill her?"

Miera's laugh rumbled through his large body. "Do you

know how many people Americans have killed in the name of freedom? Your fiancée was just one more martyr in the war that America started."

Kenneth felt the anger building inside him again. "What are you talking about? Miriam loved her country. You murdered an innocent woman!"

"No Americans are innocent," Miera interrupted. "And today all Americans will be reminded that there are those who fight against their evil ways."

"You think bombing innocent people is the answer?"

Miera frowned at Kenneth. "We are only doing to the Americans what they themselves have done to other innocents."

Miera's walkie-talkie crackled, and he pulled it from his belt. "Have you found the girl?" he asked into it.

"Yes," came the reply. "We're bringing her in."

"Don't hurt her. She has nothing to do with this," Kenneth cried out. "Just let her go, she's done nothing to you."

He was unprepared for Jorge's fist. It caught him on the jaw. "I don't take orders from you," Miera said.

Carrington stood before Kenneth. "I guess I was wrong about your motivation. I thought you wanted revenge for the death of your fiancée. Instead, you were clueless. What a waste of my resources."

Carrington gestured to Miera. "I'm done with him. Once they bring the girl, take care of them both at once."

Kenneth could hardly think straight knowing it was his fault Emma was even in danger in the first place. "Leave her out of this," he shouted, but it only earned him another punch in the face from Jorge. *Heavenly Father, please protect Emma,* he prayed silently.

Miera faced him. "Don't worry. We'll be with you shortly."

CHAPTER FOURTEEN

Emma walked meekly next to Don. "What's going to happen to me?" she asked.

"Boss'll decide that," he said, softening his grip and giving her the once-over.

Gritting her teeth, she smiled back at him. "Can't we work something out? What's your name?"

"Don," he said. "What did you have in mind?"

She ran her hand across his back. "I've seen you looking at me, what do you think I have in mind?" Her voice was smooth and inviting.

He smiled broadly and his pace quickened. "There is an office just down the hall."

Emma tried to look excited. "Wait, wait," she bit her lip. "What if Tony comes back?"

"Don't you worry about Tony," he reassured her. "I'll take care of him." He held his walkie-talkie to his lips. "Tony, I'm taking the girl to the boss. He wants you to contact the pilot and do a last check." He smiled down at Emma. "See, all taken care of."

Emma stood on her tiptoes and gave him a kiss on the cheek. "That was really smart," she praised him. He held her close and she could smell his tobacco breath and see the pockmarks underneath his five o'clock shadow. She ran her hands down his shoulders and he bent in to kiss her. The moment he touched her lips, she went into action, her hands lightning quick, grabbing the gun from the holster. She pointed it at him, shouting, "Don't move!" The movement had hurt her collarbone, but she clenched her teeth against the pain.

He held up his hands. "Do you even know how to use that thing, darlin'?" he drawled.

"Do you really believe I don't?" she said angrily, quickly taking his walkie-talkie. "Let's go for a walk, and keep your hands where I can see them."

When Don was safely tied up and locked in a cleaning closet, Emma went to find Kenneth. *Please let him be okay*, she thought.

ဢ

After what seemed like an eternity, Carrington's walkie-talkie crackled. Every muscle in Kenneth's body tensed, anticipating a report about what had happened to Emma.

"*We still can't locate her,*" the voice said.

Kenneth's spirits soared. Emma had gotten away!

Carrington looked at him calmly. "It doesn't matter," he said. "No one will know what became of you or your friend, because within an hour the bomb will be dropped over the Air Force base. We'll be long gone, but this hangar is close enough that it will be leveled. Your body will never be found."

"If we're that close to the base, the FBI probably knows you're here," Kenneth countered.

Miera laughed. "I'm quite certain that no one on the base has any clue. Why would they look right under their noses?"

"People will search for me," Kenneth said, his panic rising.

"Yes, they might be looking for you, but not for the reason you would hope," Miera said. "When your office at the firm is searched, they will find all the evidence of bribes and corruption on your computer, showing *you* were the one on the criminal path. It will look like you disappeared to avoid prison."

Miera looked at Carrington. "You'll be appropriately outraged, won't you, Edward?"

Carrington and Miera shared a brief laugh, then Carrington raised his hand. "Quiet! Did you hear something?"

Carrington pulled a small pistol from his belt and pointed it in Kenneth's direction.

The next moments were a blur as the door burst open and six armed men in bulletproof vests rushed into the room. "Drop your weapons!" one of the men yelled.

Carrington looked stunned for a moment, then turned the gun toward the agents. Before Kenneth could even blink, Mr. Carrington was shot four times in the chest. His arms flung out slowly as he fell back in his chair, a shocked expression on his face.

Jorge and Miera quickly raised their hands and dropped their guns. They were taken into custody without incident. Finally one of the agents walked over to Kenneth and asked, "Are you all right?"

Kenneth breathed deeply, trying to calm his racing heart. He averted his gaze, not wanting to look at his former boss, now dead in his chair. Kenneth stood unsteadily as the man helped untie him. Kenneth turned his back on the grisly scene. "How did you find us?" he asked the man. Before he could answer, Andrew walked in, also wearing a bulletproof vest. He spoke with one of the men, then stepped back into the hall. Within moments, Emma entered the room.

She ran to Kenneth, hugging him tightly. "Are you okay?" she asked.

Kenneth gingerly held her. "I'm fine. Are you doing all right?"

"I am now," she said, shyly looking into his eyes.

Andrew stepped beside them and said, "Emma, you're a hero."

Emma shook her head. "Oh, I wouldn't say that."

Andrew turned to Kenneth and said, "Believe me, she is. She was able to contact me and allow us to pinpoint your location. We had surrounded the perimeter, and found Emma, who led us to this room."

"What about the bomb?" Kenneth asked. "Has the plot been stopped?"

"Thankfully yes," Andrew said.

Kenneth breathed a sigh of relief. "How is everyone else? Are Julia and my grandmother all right?" he asked.

"They're fine," Andrew said. "We set the helicopter down in Jackson Hole, and they are in good hands there."

The events of the past few hours finally hit Kenneth, and he felt his legs go weak. Andrew helped him to a chair and said, "You are going to the hospital, both of you, to be checked over."

Kenneth tried to argue, but he didn't have the strength. After a few minutes they left the room and headed down the hall, but stopped when they heard a commotion coming from a closet.

"What the devil is that?" Andrew asked. He opened the door to find Don kicking himself loose from a cleaning bucket.

Don lunged for Emma, but Andrew put a gun in his ribs. "She tricked me," Don said. "She let me kiss her, then she stole my gun!"

With the help of some of the other armed men, Andrew took Don by the arms and handcuffed him.

"You let him kiss you?" Kenneth asked.

"I was trying to save you!" she said, pulling him down the

hallway. "I'll tell you about it on the way to the hospital."

As they walked onto the tarmac, it was no longer empty. Emergency vehicles were everywhere. The fighter jet was surrounded by police cars.

"Thank you, Emma. You saved my life." He put his arm around her and pulled her close, running his fingers through her long brown hair. Looking into her eyes for a moment, he bent to kiss her. "Emma," he breathed. "I—"

She put her fingers to his lips. "Kenneth, don't. Not here."

He nodded, his disappointment evident. He loved her. He knew it and wanted to tell her, but only when she was ready. They walked toward the car where Andrew was waiting with his arms folded. He didn't look happy. Kenneth knew he'd seen the attempted kiss, but he didn't care. Emma was worth any risk to him.

Andrew held the car door open for Emma, but he stopped Kenneth. "You're going in the ambulance over there."

"I don't need an ambulance," Kenneth protested.

"I'll meet you at the hospital," Emma promised.

Kenneth was surprised when another agent appeared at his side. "This way, sir," he said to Kenneth as Andrew slipped into the car. He'd planned this!

Andrew gave a slight wave to Kenneth as he and Emma drove away. Kenneth watched them, getting the distinct impression that Andrew didn't like him.

CHAPTER FIFTEEN

Kenneth's injuries were serious enough that the doctors wanted to keep him overnight for observation. Later that evening he got a pleasant surprise as his parents and other family members arrived, along with Pepper, who had been flown in from Jackson Hole. She had brought Julia with her.

They crowded into his room, anxious to hear what had happened.

Julia pushed her way through the crowd to his bed. "Hi, Kenny," Julia greeted him solemnly.

"Hey," he said. "Have you been taking care of Pepper?"

"Yeah." She gave him a small smile. "Pepper said you'd be okay if we said a prayer for you. I prayed really hard."

He helped her climb onto the bed with his good arm, where he hugged her close. "I'm so grateful you were a brave girl and kept Pepper safe."

Kenneth's parents, his sister Susan and her husband Robert joined them, making a circle around the bed.

"Mom is really mad at you," Susan announced to her brother. She reached back to take her husband's hand. "It looks like you're okay, though."

"How did you guys find out about this whole thing?"

"We had government agents at our door," his mom said. "They couldn't tell us what was going on, but needed to bring us here. I was so worried. But then Pepper was able to explain everything."

Pepper moved to the end of the bed. "I'm glad you're okay, Kenny. Julia's right. That's the hardest I've ever prayed."

Susan patted her brother's hand her eyes bright with tears. "Me, too, Kenneth." She turned into her husband's arms. "Ooh, I think we'd better go." Robert immediately reached for her coat to help her put it on.

"Where are you two going?" Kenneth asked.

Susan smiled, looked at Robert conspiratorially, who nodded back at her. "I'm going to have a baby," Susan said softly.

"Wow," Kenneth said. "My little sister is going to be a mom!" He leaned over and hugged her close. "Congratulations! That's great. At least we have some good news with all that's going on."

He shook Robert's hand, spying Emma standing near the door. "I'm so happy for you. Have you two met Emma?" He motioned for her to join them.

"Yes, she introduced herself earlier." Susan said abruptly as Emma came toward them. "I'm sorry, Kenneth, but I'm not feeling well, so we're going back to the hotel. I'm sure we'll see you later."

Kenneth's parents moved forward, his father hugging him and slapping him on the back. "Glad you're okay, son," he said.

His mother wiped her eyes. "We were so scared for you."

Kenneth shrugged. "I'm okay."

The doctor came into the room, confirming Kenneth's own diagnosis. "His wrist is fractured, and he's pretty bruised, but that seems to be the extent of his injuries. We're keeping him here overnight for observation since he was unconscious, but he'll be free to go after that."

His parents nodded, obviously relieved. "Do you want one of us to stay with you?"

Kenneth turned to Emma who had hung back behind his parents. "I'd really like Emma to stay," he said to his parents.

"Don't you think one of your parents should?" his father asked.

Pepper snorted. "He's not two years old. But Julia has missed her mother," she reminded the couple.

Kenneth's mother patted his shoulder. "We could stay with your little girl." She bent down to Julia. "My name's Kathleen. What's yours?"

"I'm Julia," the little girl replied.

Emma shook her head. "Thank you," she said. "But I think I'll go find a hotel with Julia and Pepper, and get Julia settled for the night. Then I'll come back to be with Kenneth. Is that a good compromise?" Kenneth nodded his approval.

Emma stepped to the side of the bed and bent down to kiss Kenneth on the cheek. "I'll be back soon okay?"

Kenneth took her hand. "You were my hero today. You saved us."

Emma shrugged off his praise. "I was just looking out for the people I care about, that's all."

Pepper's eyes widened slightly at Emma's words. "I had a feeling about you two," she beamed. "What exactly is going on?"

"Nothing you need to concern yourself about, Pepper. Don't scare the poor woman off," Kenneth teased. "And try to let me run my own life."

He bent forward to kiss Pepper on her cheek. "I'm glad to see you're feeling so well. I was worried about you."

Pepper took Kenneth's hand and patted it, then placed it in Emma's hand. "I know you think there's a lot of obstacles to pass before you can think of anyone in a serious way. But don't let the moment pass. Life is too short." Her eyes started to fill with tears. "I miss my Jackson every day. What I wouldn't give to have one more day with him."

"Don't upset yourself now, Pepper," Emma said anxiously. "Everything will work out how it's supposed to, you'll see."

Kenneth said goodbye to Emma and Julia, then he leaned back in his pillows. When sleep overcame him, it was a woman with deep brown eyes and long brown hair that flitted through his dreams.

The next morning Kenneth was awake early and ready to go. Emma hadn't come back to see him last night like she'd promised and he was anxious to be with her. He wanted to tell her about Miriam and the closure he'd felt when he learned the truth about her death. He wanted to tell her how grateful he was she was safe. He just wanted to be with her.

His parents had returned to be with him, and when all the paperwork had been signed, he finally settled himself in the car. "Have you seen Emma or Julia this morning?" he asked.

His parents looked at each other. "We saw Emma in the lobby this morning."

"Did she say when she might be by to see me?" No one answered. "What's going on?" he asked anxiously. "Is everything all right?"

His mother turned around to face the back seat. "She was with her father and it looked like they were checking out, although she was arguing with him over something, I couldn't quite hear what. I'm sorry, sweetie." She turned back around. "We're thinking we'll take Pepper home and spend a few days with her before we go back to Arizona. What do you think?"

Kenneth was only half-listening to her. Emma wouldn't go anywhere without saying goodbye, would she? They pulled up in front of a Days Inn in Colorado Springs to retrieve Pepper and their luggage. Kenneth stayed in the car while his parents checked out of the hotel.

"Haven't you heard anything from Emma?" Kenneth immediately asked Pepper when she reached the car.

She handed him an envelope. "Emma asked me to give this to you." Kenneth tore it open and read:

Kenneth,

I'm sorry to leave like this, but my dad really wants to spend some time with us. We're heading up to Canada and I'll be gone a few days. I'm sorry I couldn't come by last night but my dad needed to talk. Good luck with everything.

Emma

Pepper read the letter over his shoulder. "I can't believe she did that to you."

Kenneth folded the letter carefully and put it back in the envelope. "Did she mention where in Canada she was going?"

"Well, I overheard her dad talking on the phone and discussing going to Edmonton." She tilted her head. "Go after her, Kenneth."

Kenneth ran his hands through his hair. "I did want to discuss some things with her and I've wanted to go back to Canada for a while. Edmonton was in my last area on my mission. I could look up some old friends." He got out of the car, careful not to bump his wrist. "It's not like I have a job to go back to anyway."

"Good for you," Pepper said. "I'm already checked out and your parents are taking me home."

She smiled at Kenneth and continued, "I plan to use every excuse to bring up having them all move back to Utah, especially now that Susan is going to have a baby. Can you believe it? My first great-grandchild! If you all would move back to Utah, I could see everyone any time I wanted."

Pepper turned back to Kenneth. "What's your excuse for not living closer to your grandmother?"

"I don't have one. I'm not sure what I'm going to do, or where I'm going to live, at this point." He reached for her hand. "But you don't have to worry about it. I'll figure it out."

"I know a certain young lady who would be happy if you agreed to live in Utah," she responded brightly.

"Pepper," he warned. "I think we've already talked about this. My private life is just that—private. It's bad enough you know I'm going after her to Edmonton."

Pepper smiled. "Kenneth, you should know by now that there is no such thing as privacy where your grandmother is concerned. What are you waiting for? Get going."

Kenneth smiled. "I love you, Grandma," he declared, dispensing with her family pet name just once. "I need to see if there are any flights to Edmonton or if I'm renting a car."

Pepper watched him jog toward the hotel office, and it made her smile. She knew he hated to wait for anything. Even when he was a little boy, he had no patience. *Emma will be good for him,* she thought. *If only he can find her.*

CHAPTER SIXTEEN

Kenneth drove the highways of Montana like a madman. It was as if he couldn't get to Emma fast enough. He had long since driven through Idaho, just continuing north in his attempt to get to Edmonton as quickly as possible. He was disappointed that he didn't get a flight out of Colorado Springs, but the long drive was helping him think about exactly what he wanted to say to her. It also gave him time to reflect about Miriam, his sudden career change, and the abrupt U-turn his life had just taken. Would he have become an attorney if Miriam hadn't been so poorly represented? *Yes, I would have,* he thought. *I've always been fascinated by the law.* Teaching had filled something in him, but law and the intricacies of it inspired him. So did Emma. She stirred something in him he thought was long dead.

The Canadian border was now only an hour away. He was exhausted and knew he needed to stop soon. His wrist was beginning to throb, but he was avoiding taking any pain pills while he was driving. He went through the U.S.-Canada border stop without a problem and continued on, hoping to reach the city of Lethbridge before midnight. He just wanted to find a motel and get some sleep. He breathed deeply. He knew he was just inside Canada's border, but already it felt different. There was land as far as the eye could see. The familiar wheat granaries stood like sentinels watching over the farmland. The small town gas stations were deserted at this time of night, but he knew they would be bustling the next morning. Kenneth was beginning to feel in a way as if he was coming home.

His mission to Canada had been a good one. He'd baptized several families and met a lot of great people, but the real value in his mission was the testimony he had gained. Reading the scriptures every day and teaching others the gospel had changed him. He'd been a member all of his life and thought he'd had a strong testimony when he came on his mission, but actually teaching those eternal principles had strengthened his testimony immensely.

After twelve hours of driving, he found a motel with a vacancy and just went to bed in his clothes. He slept soundly, not awakening until the maid knocked on the door, telling him it was checkout time. After a quick breakfast, he continued on, anxious to reach the capital city of Edmonton.

The closer he got to the city, the more excited he became. His mind was starting to recall people and details that he'd long since forgotten. Within six hours he found himself in Edmonton, changing his money over and checking in at the Chateau Lacombe, a beautiful hotel overlooking the River Valley. He'd remembered it from his mission because of the revolving restaurant on the very top floor, La Ronde. He'd always wanted to go there during his mission, but he never could afford it on a missionary budget. *I can't really afford it now either*, he thought, *since I don't have a job*, but it was too much of a temptation. He went to the check-in desk to reserve a room.

When he was in his room, he took off his jacket and got out the phone book. There was only one number listed for the CSIS office. When he called it he got a recording of the field office hours and address. After a quick shower, he drove down there. He walked through the glass doors emblazoned with a crest of a maple leaf surrounded by what looked like blue flower petals, topped off with a crown. The office area looked like any other office with desks, computers, and men and women in suits busily milling around. He walked over to the reception desk, where a small woman with glasses greeted him. "May I help you?"

"Yes, I'm looking for one of your directors, Andrew Blythe," Kenneth said pleasantly.

"One moment please," she said. She spoke into a telephone announcing that Mr. Blythe had a guest. "Just wait over there," she instructed.

Kenneth sat down on a small reception couch. In a few moments a man in a suit stood in front of him. "Follow me," he said.

Kenneth was ushered to a small office with two stainless steel hard back chairs facing a long table.

"Can I ask what you would like to see Mr. Blythe about?" the man asked.

"It's personal business," Kenneth replied.

"Uh, huh," the man said, drawing his eyebrows together. He didn't take his eyes off Kenneth. "Mr. Blythe is currently unavailable. Perhaps if you leave your name and a number where you can be reached . . ."

Kenneth turned to face him head on. "It is important that I speak to him. Can you tell him that?"

The other agent handed Kenneth a pad of paper and pencil. Kenneth scribbled down his hotel room number and a phone number. The agent briefly looked at it, then again at Kenneth. "Okay, I'll be sure Mr. Blythe gets your message." He opened the door and escorted Kenneth back to the reception area.

"You'll be sure he gets that?" Kenneth asked.

"He probably won't be available until Monday," the agent said softly, then he escorted Kenneth to the lobby before disappearing down the hall. Kenneth sighed. This wasn't going as he had planned. Well, if he had until Monday, he might as well hit some of his old mission spots.

The missionaries' favorite destination on P-day was West Edmonton Mall, so he headed there first. West Edmonton Mall was one of the largest tourist attractions in Alberta and he was anxious to see how it had grown since he'd been there last. It covered 48 city blocks, housing 800 stores with over 100 places to eat. He entered in the far entrance, near the pirate ship that offered submarine rides to see the marine life. He watched the dolphins for a moment, then moved on to the five-acre water park to see the wave pool and water slides, with all the people enjoying themselves. *The bungee jumpers are crazy,* he thought. *I wouldn't be caught dead doing something like that.*

He strolled along the main floor, to the ice palace where the Edmonton Oilers hockey team was practicing. He watched in fascination the smooth drills the coach put the men through. Hockey fans were lined up at the side of the rink, waiting for autographs and a glimpse of their favorite players. After a few moments he moved on, staring at all the changes that had been made. Adventure Golf, the eighteen hole mini-golf park, had been totally redone. Galaxy Land, the indoor amusement park now had a haunted castle and a fun house in addition to the MindBender roller coaster and giant swing. *Julia would love this,* he thought quietly observing the families there.

After an hour of wandering around, he stopped in front of a store that sold pianos and organs. Suddenly a name popped into Kenneth's mind. *James Hinson.* Kenneth shook his head. *Wow, I haven't thought of him in years. I wonder if he's still in the area.*

Kenneth went back to the hotel, changing into some navy

blue Dockers and a cream three-button shirt. He grabbed the phone book and looked up James Hinson, hoping he still lived in the same house. He did.

The first time they'd met, Brother Hinson had introduced himself to the missionaries before they had even gotten into the foyer. He was a tall man, with small round glasses over a rather pointy nose. He was trim with lots of dark hair, cut short in a military style, but it was his smile that endeared him to people. It was large and revealed beautiful white teeth. He was a recent convert, he had explained, and was still single at thirty-five.

He loved the missionaries that had taught him so much that he decided to take all future missionaries in the area under his wing. He was so anxious for Kenneth and his companion to come to dinner at his home and wanted to be the first to invite them, so he had come early to church to make sure he was the first. Kenneth and his companion had gratefully accepted.

When the missionaries found his home, they knocked and Brother Hinson had practically pulled them inside. In the entire time Kenneth had known him, he was always excitable, wanting to show everything to everyone, especially his prized possession. His entire living room was taken up by a large organ and two large speakers on either side.

Brother Hinson had grinned widely at their expressions, explaining that he had saved the organ from a church that was being torn down. They had given him the whole thing, speakers and all. He'd had to buy his own home so he could practice, since it wouldn't fit in his apartment. He loved to play on it and his dream was to someday perform on the organ in the Tabernacle in Utah.

As a convert, he loved the gospel immensely. His face always showed his enthusiasm for the restoration and reverence he had for the Savior. Kenneth couldn't wait to see him.

Kenneth considered calling first, but the Hinson home wasn't far away. *I'd rather surprise him,* Kenneth thought. He wasted no time and quickly drove to James's house. He walked up to the white home, remembering how many times his missionary shoes had walked this walk. He knocked firmly on the door and it was opened by a blonde woman holding a wriggling toddler.

"Hello, I must have the wrong house," he began. "I'm looking for James Hinson."

The woman looked him over and smiled. "You don't have the wrong house. I'm his wife Josie. Let me get him for you."

Brother Hinson came to the door, looking much the same as he had ten years ago, except his dark hair now had gray in it. He was cleaning his glasses and when he put them on and looked at Kenneth, his face broke into a huge grin.

"Elder King!" he practically shouted, enveloping Kenneth in a big bear hug.

It had been so long since anyone had called him "Elder." He slapped him on the back. "Brother Hinson, you haven't changed a bit."

"Come in, come in. I see you've met my wife Josie." He took the toddler from her arms. "And this is our little Jared."

Kenneth laughed. "Doesn't it ever tongue tie you with so many J's in the family?"

"No, we purposely did it like that. We're carrying on a tradition from my family," he replied, looking at his wife.

"That's right," Kenneth snapped his fingers. "Your parents and brothers and sisters were all J names, weren't they? I'd almost forgotten."

James ticked his fingers off. "My parents are Jack and JoAnn, my three brothers are Jayden, Jeffrey, Jonathan, and my sister is Jacqueline." He smiled proudly.

Josie looked at Kenneth, seemingly impressed he'd

remembered the J name tradition. "How long has it been since you've seen each other?"

Brother Hinson looked at Kenneth. "It's been a little over ten years, hasn't it?"

Kenneth shook his head in disbelief. "That's right. I can hardly believe it's been that long."

"I seem to remember someone promising to write," James said, raising his eyebrows.

"I know. I'm sorry." Kenneth held up his hands. "I went home, eventually became a lawyer, moved to Phoenix and started working as a criminal defense attorney."

Now it was James's turn to be impressed. "Wow, that must be interesting work. Do you enjoy it?"

"Definitely," he said, then smoothly changed the subject, wanting to hear about James. "So when did you get married? How old is your little guy?"

Josie reached for James's hand. "We've been married eight years now, and Jared is three and a half. Our little baby is asleep in the other room. Her name is Jessica. She's eight months old."

"I just can't believe you got married," Kenneth exclaimed, then realized how that must have sounded. "I mean, I just didn't think . . ."

James laughed at the expression on Kenneth's face. "I know what you mean. When you're still single at thirty-five, you wonder if you'll ever get married." He looked tenderly at Josie. "I guess I just had to wait for the right person." He started to tickle Jared. "And now I'm the luckiest man on the face of the planet."

"Wow, married with two kids. Who would have thought?" He looked over at the organ, still the centerpiece of the living room. "I see she didn't make you get rid of the organ."

Josie smiled. "He plays for the children at bedtime so they can go to sleep."

Kenneth looked at her incredulously. "They can sleep through that?"

She nodded. "They love it."

"Did you ever make it to Utah, to play on the Tabernacle organ?"

James shook his head. "No, but I'm going to one day."

After a few more minutes of chatting, Kenneth stood to go. "I should probably let you get back to what you were doing."

"Hold on," James said. "We can't let you run off so soon. Stay and have dinner with us." Both Josie and James looked at him, wanting him to stay.

Kenneth finally agreed. "Remember all those dinners you cooked for me and my companions?" he asked. "You were a great cook."

James looked over his shoulder as he started for the kitchen. "Wait until you taste Josie's cooking. She is wonderful. We made perogies tonight."

Kenneth remembered the native Ukrainian food, and his mouth watered. It had been a long time since he had tasted one. "I can't wait."

He ended up staying until midnight, telling all the old mission stories to Josie. Kenneth got caught up on old companions that James had heard from and he also got hear about the Hinsons' courtship and marriage. It admittedly sent Kenneth's thoughts back to Emma.

James asked if he'd had time to look anyone else up and Kenneth said he hadn't. James invited him to church the next day at the old ward and Kenneth decided to go. It was a good feeling to be back among friends.

He returned to the hotel but neglected to set the alarm. He overslept and had to rush to make it to the chapel on time. It was a twenty minute drive from the hotel, and traffic was terrible. He finally made it and strode through the foyer, just

as they were finishing the opening hymn. He stopped in the
doorway and was looking for a seat in the back, while the bishop
was making announcements. He stopped at the sound of the
familiar voice announcing new callings in the ward. He looked
over at the man behind the pulpit. *Could it be?* Kenneth asked
himself. *Yes! Brother Gray is the bishop!*

Elias Gray had been his last baptism before he went home.
He had taken the missionary lessons many times and several sets
of missionaries had tried to help him into the waters of baptism,
but they had all gone home disappointed. When Kenneth was
put into the area, his companion had set up more appointments
with Mr. Gray, but had told Kenneth, that Gray was a lost cause.
"He just likes to visit with the missionaries and try to trip us
up."

Kenneth had gone along, just to see what the guy was like.
He had long hair, wore two gold chains around his neck that
contrasted with the multi-colored tie dye shirt he wore, and
he smoked like a chimney. He invited the missionaries in and
after a brief introduction to Kenneth, he had given his own
introduction. "My parents were Bible-thumpers, named all their
kids after people in the Bible and kept strict rules on us. We
couldn't make a move without consulting the Good Book first."
He had puffed away on his cigarette. "When I turned eighteen
I got out of there and never looked back. I did everything my
parents had ever told me not to, and I like my life."

They had visited him for weeks, teaching him the discussions
again and discussing scriptures. Elias had an excellent knowledge
of the Bible and enjoyed comparing the Book of Mormon
scriptures to Bible verses. "It's amazing that Joseph Smith was
even able to translate the book," he'd said on a number of
occasions, his words showing his burgeoning testimony. During
their conversations, Kenneth realized the only thing holding
Elias back from baptism was his Word of Wisdom problem and

the fact that he had never asked his Heavenly Father if the Book of Mormon was from God.

He confronted Elias one day. "How many times have you read the Book of Mormon now?"

"'Five or six, I imagine." Still puffing away on his cigarette, he had eyed Kenneth suspiciously. "Why?"

"How many times have you kneeled in prayer to ask if it was true?" he went on doggedly.

Elias had just puffed away for a few moments. "None."

"Why not?"

He wouldn't answer the question and had abruptly asked them to leave. Kenneth had gone home feeling like he was a terrible missionary. It was his job to give opportunities to people to feel the Spirit, not to challenge them. They had gone back to visit Elias several times that next week, but he wouldn't speak to them. After three weeks of waiting and trying, he finally let the missionaries back in. He had cut his hair, taken off his jewelry and was wearing clean jeans, and a clean T-shirt, was without his cigarettes and holding his Book of Mormon in his hand. "How soon can I be baptized?"

Kenneth had almost fallen over in shock. Elias had told them how after they had left that night, he had gone to his room and prayed. He wrestled with his feelings for weeks, fearing the idea of getting involved with organized religion again after his upbringing. He knew the Book of Mormon was inspired, but he was afraid to ask for a witness, because then he knew he would have to join the church if he knew it was true. He'd prayed as earnestly as he knew how and the witness had come. He'd been truly converted, his testimony strengthened, and to top it all off, he'd stopped smoking. "I'm ready for baptism," he had declared.

They had set his baptism date for a few weeks away and finished up all the loose ends of interviews and requirements. It had been a great day when Elias Gray was baptized. Kenneth had felt on top of the world, knowing he had been an instrument in helping Brother Gray find his eternal destiny.

And here he was the bishop, Kenneth thought. *You couldn't find a better man to serve the people.* He found a seat and sat down for the service. After the meeting one of the families that he had baptized recognized him and came over to talk.

Kenneth couldn't believe how their children had grown. Greg Abbott had been nine when he'd left and now was ready to go on his mission. He laughed with Greg's mother Lisa over how Greg used to look up to Kenneth, worrying if he would ever get taller. Now Greg matched him in height, but probably outweighed him by twenty pounds. He just couldn't believe how everyone had changed.

He could see Bishop Gray making his way toward him. He waded through the wave of people heading for the doors and finally reached Elias. "How have you been?"

Elias enveloped him in a giant hug. "The missionary who converted me has come back to the fold. How are you doing?"

Kenneth smiled. "I'm fine. It's good to be here. It feels like home," he said motioning to the family still behind him.

"What brings you this far north?"

"Oh, just here for a visit," he replied vaguely.

Elias looked at him closely. "Maybe we should have a talk in my office after church today, eh?"

Kenneth laughed now that the shoe was on the other foot. Now it was Elias wanting to dish out advice to him. "I'd love to visit with you, Bishop."

"I'll plan it."

Kenneth didn't get a chance to say much else to Elias after that, since every few feet, someone else needed to talk to the Bishop. He found his way to Sunday School and sat down. It was a good lesson on obedience and Kenneth even had a few comments. He sat with James in priesthood and just enjoyed the feeling of brotherhood that he had never truly felt at the law firm.

After church, he waited patiently for Elias to clear his schedule so they could talk uninterrupted for a while.

"Come on in, Elder King. Have a seat." He motioned toward the chair on the opposite side of the desk. He sat down in his comfortable black swivel chair. He steepled his fingers on the desk. "What can I do for you?" he asked.

Kenneth shifted in his chair trying to get comfortable. "What do you mean? I'm fine."

Elias looked at him knowingly. "Don't think you can get away with that in my office, Elder. I know something is going on with you to just show up here after all this time."

Kenneth averted his eyes and stared at the pictures of the Savior on the walls of the office. One of his favorite paintings showing the Savior knocking on a knobless door, was prominently displayed. Maybe it would help to confide in someone.

He smiled and took a deep breath. "Two of the senior partners in my law firm were killed, I lost my job because my firm was involved in helping a terrorist plan a bomb attack on the United States, and I'm in love with someone, but now I can't find her."

Elias leaned back. "Whew, I can't believe you said all that in one breath. How can I help?"

Kenneth looked up. "You can't. I'm just waiting for Monday so I can find out where Emma went, then I'm going home to look for a new job."

"Sure you don't want to move to Canada and work here? I remember how much you loved skiing. Lake Louise isn't too far away, you know."

Kenneth laughed. "How can you remember that?"

He leaned across the desk, resting his head on his hand.

"I remember a lot of things about you. You always had this spiritual attitude that I liked—not too pushy, just peaceful. Don't let the world take that away from you. I know what that's like. I've been there."

Kenneth smiled at the memory of Elias in his tie-dye and gold necklaces. "I remember."

Elias pointed his finger at him. "Hey, that's not what I meant."

The two men laughed. Elias bent and pulled a picture out of his top drawer. It was him on his baptism day, standing in white next to Kenneth. "Next to my wedding day, this was the happiest day of my life. I keep the picture close by so I can remember how far I've come since then."

After looking at himself in his younger days for a moment, Kenneth handed back the picture. "Those were the days, weren't they?"

"So tell me, who is this girl you're in love with?"

Kenneth ran his hands through his hair. "Her name is Emma. She's smart, beautiful, and has a wonderful daughter. Everything I ever could have asked for."

"That's great. But why haven't you married before now?" the bishop asked, looking puzzled. "With all those girls you were writing to during your mission, I thought at least one of them would snag you."

He shook his head. "I was engaged once, but my fiancée was murdered." It felt so different to be able to say murdered rather than committed suicide. It didn't hurt as much somehow, knowing that she had been trying to do the right thing when she was killed.

"Kenneth, I am so sorry," Elias said, a look of sympathy on his face.

"Thanks. Anyway, after that I was busy teaching, then I

decided to go to law school and then I was busy practicing law," he added.

"So you've been busy practicing law and now you have no job and a woman you love that you can't find. Are you wondering what to do with yourself?"

"Partly." He rubbed his hand over his chin. "What do you think I should do?"

"This is so wild, that you would be asking me, when you practically ordered me to get down on my knees and pray. My advice is to take your own advice, Elder King," he said firmly. "When was the last time you prayed to find direction? You've made your way in the world, maybe it's time to find your way to eternity." He pointed his finger at the picture behind Kenneth. "The Lord is waiting for you to ask, so he can bless you. I know that for a fact."

He looked back at the picture, then stood to leave. "Thanks. As always, you've given me a lot to think about."

"Are you going to speak to me again?" He held out his hand.

Kenneth took it and shook firmly. "Of course. Let's meet for lunch while I'm here."

"That sounds great." Elias moved toward the door. "How about tomorrow?"

"Are you sure you can take that much of me in two days?" he chuckled.

"Listen, if I can put up with you when you were a cocky missionary, I can put up with anything you can throw at me now." He hugged Kenneth. "I'll see you tomorrow."

Lisa and Greg Abbott were waiting for him when he emerged from the office, insisting he come over for Sunday dinner. He agreed since he was eager to catch up with one of the families he had baptized.

He had met them tracting and Mrs. Abbott had let them in.

They had just buried their oldest son Luke, who had been hit by a car when he was walking home from elementary school. When the missionaries taught the family about eternal life and being together as a family forever, Mrs. Abbott cried. Her testimony had grown and before long her husband, Sam, was also taking the discussions. The other children, Greg and Rebecca, were ten and nine at the time, so the missionaries became fast friends to the children. They had been a fun family to teach.

The Abbotts welcomed Kenneth warmly, treating him even better than they did when he was a missionary.

"Are you ready to go on your mission, Greg?" Kenneth asked. "It makes me feel ancient that you're old enough to serve a mission."

Greg smiled excitedly, helping Kenneth set the table. "I can't wait to go. I've never been anywhere outside of Canada and I've always wanted to see France. My farewell is next week and we'll travel down to Utah the next day." He set down a fork. "Maybe you can stay for my farewell."

Lisa walked in carrying a plate of roast beef. "How long are you here for, Elder King?"

Kenneth smiled again, not used to being called that. "You can call me Kenneth, you know."

"That's right, I had forgotten your name!" she said incredulously. "Remember how hard I tried to get it out of you and all you would say was 'Elder' until the day you left for home?" She cocked her head. "You do look like a Kenneth."

The family hadn't changed a bit. Dinner time was full of fun and laughter, teasing Rebecca about her new boyfriend and telling tall tales of mission life. It was hard to go, but Kenneth finally said his goodbyes around midnight.

He went back to the hotel. Driving back he thought of the lives he had touched as a missionary and how different his life had been then. So much more simple. Seeing their lives now made him want to re-evaluate his own life and where it was going. What was it Elias had said? When was the last time he had prayed for direction? He got ready for bed and knelt down. His mind was blank for a moment and then he just started to pour his heart out to his Heavenly Father, asking fervently for his help. When he rose and climbed into bed, he hadn't received any bolt of lightning, but he knew he was one step closer to finding out where he should be.

The next day he went back to the CSIS field office but was told Mr. Blythe wouldn't be there until the afternoon. He met Elias for lunch at Cucci's, just catching up and enjoying being together. Elias didn't mention their conversation in the bishop's office again until they said goodbye. "Remember, Kenneth, the Lord loves you. He gives us trials to help us learn."

Kenneth smiled ruefully. "I must really need to learn a few things."

"Keep praying. He has all the answers. I can never repay you for all you did for me. Just know that I'll be forever grateful you were in tune with the Spirit that day."

Kenneth watched him walk down the street, touched by his caring. While he was waiting for the appointed time when Andrew would supposedly be available he took a drive over to the Edmonton Temple. The grounds were beautiful and well-kept, and a feeling a peace permeated the air. He sat down on the small bench, just looking at the temple spires. He began to pray, really wanting to know that direction Heavenly Father would have him go in. The answer came so forcefully, Kenneth could not deny it. He left the temple grounds, determined to follow his answer, and returned to the field office.

CHAPTER SEVENTEEN

Kenneth made it to the office prepared to demand to see Andrew. Instead, he was ushered right back to the first room he'd been escorted to. Andrew was waiting for him there, sitting in a chair his arms folded.

Before Kenneth could speak, Andrew held up his hands. "She's not here, she's gone back to Utah."

Kenneth took a deep breath. "Did you tell her I was here?"

Andrew shook his head. "No, I didn't."

"Why?"

"Because I wanted to talk to you first. My daughter has been through too much for you to be playing with her feelings and vulnerabilities."

Kenneth looked at him incredulously. "Are you kidding? I love Emma, I would never play with her emotions."

Andrew snorted. "How could you grow to love her when you've only known her for two weeks?"

"We've lived a lifetime in those two weeks, sir," Kenneth said. "I know you don't know me very well, but I am in love with your daughter and I plan to marry her, if she'll have me."

Andrew stared at him, his arms still folded. "Do you plan to ask me for her hand in marriage?"

Kenneth licked his lips, not taking his eyes off Andrew. "Sir, may I have your permission to ask Emma to marry me?"

Andrew stood up and came around the table to stand in front of Kenneth. "Yes, you have my permission to marry my daughter."

Kenneth jerked his head up to look at Andrew. "What?"

"You have my permission to marry Emma, if you can get her to agree," he smiled. "I just had to make sure your feelings for her were as strong as her feelings are for you." He held out his hand to Kenneth who stood to shake it. "I practically had to drag her here, and all she talked about was you, hoping you were okay and understood about her leaving. She tried calling you at Pepper's, but no one answered. I was going to tell her where you were this morning, but she left so early that I wasn't even up." He shrugged his shoulders. "She's headstrong like her mother was."

Kenneth patted his shoulder. "Thanks Andrew. I won't let you down."

Andrew escorted him to the reception area. "I'm not going to be able to contact Emma for a while. Could you let her know I'm sorry about not telling her where you were. I really had planned to." He stopped. "And tell her I love her."

Kenneth smiled, a little chill of déja vú going through him. "I will," he said.

"Good luck," Andrew waved as he went through the door.

"I'll need it," Kenneth murmured.

CHAPTER EIGHTEEN

As soon as Emma got home, she went to Pepper's, but no one knew where Kenneth was. Pepper told her he'd gone to Edmonton after her, but apparently hadn't been able to find her. "Don't worry," Pepper consoled. "He'll find you."

Emma tried not to think about it, and just be grateful he was safe and healthy. *And that he's looking for you,* her heart whispered. She forced her life to go back to routine. She went to work, and Julia went to school. The days ended up being filled with many important tasks, but she still couldn't stop thinking about Kenneth. Julia asked about him incessantly, wondering where he was. It was exasperating when she was wondering the same thing and frustrated that she didn't know the answer. She wanted to call Kenneth's parents, but she didn't know their number in Arizona and she didn't want to seem too forward. She was sure Kenneth would call when he was ready.

❧

Kenneth drove into Pepper's driveway, exhausted from the trip, but happier than he had ever been. He wanted to go straight to Emma's, but knew with the lateness of the hour he had to wait. *She was probably in bed anyway,* he thought. He went to Pepper's, using the extra keys she had given him. Grabbing his luggage he went into the house, wistfully hoping Pepper had left some of her baked goods out for him. He set his bags down, and went to the kitchen. It was in perfect order, with an apple pie in the fridge. He took it out and cut himself a large slice. Eating it slowly, he planned everything he wanted to say to Emma tomorrow. He finally finished his pie and shut off the light. Stopping by Pepper's room, he looked in to find her reading in bed. She patted the covers.

"I'm glad you made it back," she said. "Have you seen Emma yet?"

"No," he replied. "But I'm going to tomorrow."

"Do you know what you're going to say?"

He winked at his grandmother. "I'm a lawyer, aren't I? Emma just needs to be persuaded to see my point of view." He got up. "I'm heading to bed, I'll see you in the morning."

₮

Emma decided to take Julia to the park. It was getting warmer and she needed a break from work. She bundled up and packed two sack lunches and headed for the playground. It was a warm day, but when the wind blew, it got chilly. She pulled Julia's hat down. "One more slide, sweetie and then we should go."

Julia looked up at her mother, her cheeks rosy and eyes bright. "Just a little longer, Mommy?"

She crouched down. "Mommy's almost done with a very big project, and then we can come to the park every day."

She watched Julia go down the slide and they walked slowly to the car. "I miss Kenny," Julia said plaintively.

Emma sighed. They'd had this same conversation many times

in the past few days. "I do, too, sweetie."

"When is he coming back?" she asked.

"I don't know," she replied.

"Can we go visit Pepper? Maybe she knows."

She picked Julia up. "Not today, okay?" She buckled her in the car.

"Do you think Kenny will come and see us again?" she asked, watching the cars and houses pass by on the way home.

"I don't know if he'll come see us again, honey," she said as she pulled into the driveway. "I hope so."

She parked and started around the car to unbuckle Julia. When they got into the house the phone was ringing. It was the agent assigned to the Miera case giving her an update. He told her Miera was being questioned and would be put on trial as an enemy of the state. "The evidence on that disk will be extremely vital to the case," he droned. Emma hung up the phone feeling satisfied. *At least Paul's life hadn't been totally in vain,* she thought.

છ

"Pepper I'm going out," Kenneth called.

His grandmother came to the front entrance as Kenneth was tying his shoe. "Wait," she said. "I've got something for you."

She held a small wooden jewelry box his grandfather had made Pepper for their wedding day. Her name was painstakingly carved in the top. She opened it and drew out a ring.

Holding it out to him, she took a deep breath. "Kenny, this ring symbolized a pure love between two people." A silent tear ran down her cheek. "I know you've found that with Emma. Put this to good use when you feel ready."

He handed her his handkerchief and she sniffled into it. "Remember the past, but look forward to the future, my boy."

She reached up to hug him. "I love you, you know."

She's always known what I was thinking, he thought. "Don't worry, Pepper, I'm ready to put the past behind me." He hugged her small frail body. "I love you, too."

CHAPTER NINETEEN

Emma rubbed her eyes. She was so tired the words on the page were swimming and merging on the pages. Trying to re-codify the city ordinance had been a huge task. She yawned, tired from being up most of the night. She slid off her bed and trudged to the shower, hoping that would wake her up.

The shower revived her somewhat, but her brain was just overloaded. The sooner she got the document approved the better. Then she could relax and take a break with Julia for a while. She felt like she hadn't even been among the land of the living lately, stopping only to eat and sleep occasionally.

She packed her briefcase with a myriad of files, hoping she had everything. After getting Julia's breakfast, and packing her backpack, she loaded her in the car and dropped her off at kindergarten, then went straight to work. Traffic was light and she made it to work quickly. Hardly anyone was in the building yet besides her assistant, who grinned at her. Emma creased her brow. "Hi, June."

"Hi, Emma," she said, almost giggling.

Emma gave her a puzzled look, closing the door to her office and sitting down at her desk, taking out her files. She jumped when a familiar voice said softly in her ear, "Hi, Emma."

She jumped. "You scared me!" She turned to look up at Kenneth, not able to keep the smile off of her face. "How did you get in here?"

"I've been waiting for you."

She stood on her toes and hugged him. "How are you?" she asked, glad to see him beside her.

He reached for her hand. "I'm a lot better now. How's Julia?"

"She's fine. What are you doing here?" She sat on the edge of the desk.

"I called your offices and your assistant told me when she expected you in." His thumb lightly caressed her ring finger. "We need to talk."

Her stomach fluttered a little. His hair was perfectly done today except for the small curls near his ears. *I wonder if he usually has those cut off*, she mused. Then she realized he was looking at her as if waiting for an answer. "What did you say?"

He had a determined look. "I said we need to talk."

"About what?" she asked mildly.

"About us," he almost growled. "About what happened, about where you've been."

"Kenneth, I'm sorry about leaving, my dad . . ." she started.

Kenneth held up his hand. "I know. I followed you to Edmonton and I had a great discussion with your dad."

"You did?"

"Yes, I think we have an understanding." He caressed her cheek. "I looked up some of the people I'd met on my mission, visited the temple, thought about a lot of things. I'd like to tell you about it."

The warmth in his eyes sent tingles down her spine. "I'd like that."

June knocked at the door. "Emma, sorry, but the mayor needs you to look at this right away."

Kenneth let his hand drop. "I'll wait for you after work. Then we can go somewhere and talk."

"Okay," she said, not wanting to part so soon. "You'll wait for me? I should be done around noon. Then I can take a break."

"Yes," he reassured. "I'll be right outside when you're done. Good luck today."

Emma could hardly think of all the work that needed to be done as she watched him walk away. Her spirit soared. How could she work today when she was in love? She smiled. *There,* she admitted to herself. *I love Kenneth King.* Now if only he loved her back. The young woman began to speak to her, telling her exactly what the mayor wanted, but all she heard was Kenneth telling her he'd be waiting.

Kenneth met her outside her office as he had promised. He helped her into his car and they started to drive. "Did you get that project finished up?" he asked.

"Yes, finally. I don't know if being a city attorney is really what I thought it would be. I miss the excitement of prosecution sometimes." She didn't look at him, just stared out the window.

"I'm sure you are fine," he reassured.

"Where are we going?"

"It's a surprise." He reached over and took her hand.

She turned and smiled at him. "After the last two weeks, I hate surprises. Tell me where we're going."

He chuckled. He could understand her feelings. "We're going to the Orem courthouse."

"Why?" she asked.

"I want to show you something," he told her with a twinkle in his eye.

She grinned. "I don't know if I like the sound of that."

They pulled up in front of the old courthouse. It was a plain brown brick building with a staircase that could be plainly seen through the windows. They walked through the front doors and he led her to the second floor. The large double doors to the right had a sign that said *Court Officers Only*, and he led her through there.

"Kenneth, I don't think we're supposed to be in here," she said, looking around as if waiting for someone to stop them.

"It's okay, Emma. I cleared it." He took her hand and led her through the chairs and past the attorney desks. He helped her sit down at the witness stand.

"What's going on? Am I supposed to be a witness?" she demanded lightly.

Kenneth walked back behind the defense attorney's desk. "Yes," he replied simply. "I don't think I have to put you under oath for this, but I expect you to tell the truth."

Emma shifted in her seat, a bewildered look on her face. "Okay." She brightened. "Is this because you want to show off your trial skills?"

He scowled. "No, but I instruct the witness to only speak when a question has been asked."

She motioned as if she was zipping her lips. "Yes, sir."

"Now, earlier this month, did you meet the grandson of Penelope Davis at a fast food joint called the Purple Turtle and then in a church kitchen?"

"Yes, I did."

"Can you tell us about that meeting at the church?" He walked around the table, leaning against it.

"I walked into the room and this strange man was coming toward my squealing daughter who was trying to get away from him."

"And what was your reaction?"

"I rescued my daughter from him."

Kenneth frowned. "Was he hurting her?"

She smiled at the frown. "No, in fact I believe he was trying to wash her face."

"Did you ever spend time with this man other than that incident?"

Emma blushed and Kenneth chuckled at the reaction. "The witness is instructed to answer."

"Yes, I spent time with that man. We've gone driving together, he's helped me with work and he saved my life once."

"Are you grateful to him for allegedly saving your life?"

"Yes," she replied softly.

"Do you know how grateful he is to you for returning the favor and saving his life from a known terrorist?" he asked expectantly. He stood a few feet in front of her trying to gauge her reaction. His look softened. "Do you know how I feel about you?"

Emma shifted again looking uncomfortable. "I object to the question's relevance and the defense attorney is leading the witness."

Kenneth walked over to stand before her in the witness stand. "But your honor, the question is very relevant since the defense attorney wants to lead the witness." He took both hands in hers, looking into those eyes that he could drown in. "I m— mean... " He stammered a little, not at all like him. He squared his shoulders. "I love you with all my heart, Emma James, and I want to marry you. I want to be a father to your daughter, I want to be with you for as long as I draw breath." He fished in his pocket and presented her with Pepper's ring.

He walked around to the side of the wooden stand and got down on one knee. "Emma, will you marry me?"

A silent tear rolled down her cheek. "I can't believe it," she breathed.

Kenneth was so nervous he could hardly stand it. "Is that a yes?" he asked hesitantly.

"Yes," she almost whispered, then threw her arms around him. "Definitely yes!" she shouted.

Kenneth stood and took her left hand, slipping the engagement ring on her finger. He bent close to her and whispered, "I love you," before he sealed the sentiment with a kiss.

The door opened and a court clerk peeked her head in and smiled. "I see the case has been settled, counselor."

"Yes," they replied in unison.

She closed the door, leaving the couple alone. "Maybe I'd better ask Julia," he said, realizing he probably should have done that first.

"She's going to be so happy. She hasn't stopped asking about you since you left. It was driving me crazy." She tilted her face to look up at him.

He couldn't resist, kissing her again. "Well, at least she kept me in your thoughts."

"You were never far away."

Another clerk poked her head in. "I think it's time to go," he said ruefully.

They held hands all the way to the car, with Kenneth rubbing the new ring on her finger. He still couldn't believe she'd said yes. He'd never felt so happy in all his life.

They made it to the house in record time, excited to tell Julia the news. Emma paid the babysitter and took Julia into the living room where Kenneth was waiting. As soon as Julia saw Kenneth she ran into his arms, giving him a tight hug. "Kenny, I missed you!"

He laughed. "I missed you, too."

"Honey, his name is Kenneth. You should call him Kenneth," she chided her daughter.

Kenneth held up his hand. "Do you know that Pepper is the only other person to ever call me Kenny? I think it's right that you have that privilege, too, don't you?"

Kenneth turned her so she was facing him and squatted down to be at eye level with her. "Julia, I have a special question I want to ask you. How would you feel if I married your mommy and came and lived with you?"

She hugged him again. "If you marry my mommy, won't you be my daddy?"

"Yes, he'll be your daddy," Emma confirmed.

Julia jumped off Kenneth's lap. "Hooray! That would be great. I love you, Kenny," she said as she threw her arms around him. "I'm lucky because you tell really good stories about bunnies and little girls," she bubbled happily. "Mom, can I go tell Nathan?"

"Sure, honey," she said. Emma helped Julia get her shoes on and helped her cross the road. When she was safely at Nathan's she walked back to the house. Kenneth was waiting for her on the couch.

Emma sat down sighing heavily. "I need to tell you something Kenneth." She moved away slightly, as if she needed to tell him in her own space. "When Paul and I were married I trusted him completely and when he didn't want our baby it devastated me. I felt like I couldn't trust anyone." Kenneth could see she was trying to maintain her composure. "When the missionaries taught me about eternal marriage, I never thought it would happen to me. Who would want a woman with a child? I didn't trust my judgment anymore. But look where I am today." She looked quickly at Kenneth as if gauging his reaction. "I just have to ask. Can you really handle an instant family?" She twirled a small piece of hair.

He gathered her in his arms. "I wouldn't have it any other way. I love you and Julia."

Emma smiled, and snuggled deeper in his arms. "I was hoping you'd say that. I can't believe it. I just can't believe it."

She turned in his arms and reached up for a kiss. "I love you."

He sighed, happy to hear the words. "Do you want to be sealed to me for eternity?"

She creased her forehead, as if thinking it over. Then her face broke into a large, beautiful smile. "More than anything."

He hugged the woman in his arms tightly, his own tears starting to fall. "Are you sure?"

"Yes," she replied simply.

"Well, I should probably warn you," he said, smelling the sweetness of her hair. "I have this problem."

Her shoulders shook with her laughter. "Really?"

"I hate waiting. Ever since I was a little boy, I could never wait for anything and I haven't changed."

"So?" she asked. "What are you saying?"

"How long do you want me to wait to marry you?"

She turned in his arms to face him. "Will you marry me in August?"

He smiled. "Definitely."

⁂

Emma awoke early, then rested in her bed for a moment. Today was her wedding day to Kenneth. She could hardly believe how quickly the last four months had flown by. It had gone a lot smoother than she had thought it would. They had spent practically every day of their engagement together, getting to know one another better, and making memories to last a lifetime. Kenneth had started his own law firm in Utah County and it seemed to be going well. It made Emma miss being a prosecutor sometimes seeing how excited he got about some of his cases.

Her father had finally been able to contact her and when she told him her news he seemed to be glad she was moving on in her life and wouldn't be alone. Kenneth's parents had been thrilled from the beginning. Susan had taken a while to warm up, but Emma thought that was probably part of being sick with the pregnancy. She had seemed more friendly as the wedding had gotten closer and her pregnancy progressed. Of course, Pepper had taken credit for the whole thing.

Her bedroom door opened and Julia did a running leap for her bed. "Hi, Mom."

She hugged her daughter. "Did you have a good sleep?"

"We're getting married today," she announced.

Emma laughed. "We *are* getting married today. Are you happy?"

Julia nodded her head. "Yes." She looked at her bridesmaid dress hanging on her mother's closet door. "I'm going to look beautiful."

Emma was just about to answer, but it was then, sitting on her bed in her darkened room holding her daughter that the most comforting feeling came over her. She could feel the warmth of the Spirit and knew without a doubt that she was doing the right thing. "Kenneth and I love you very much, Julia," she murmured, hesitant to break the mood.

"I love you, too," she answered back, her little arms squeezing tight around Emma's neck. "Let's get married."

ಇ

Kneeling across the altar, Kenneth looked into the mirrors that reflected Emma and himself going on for eternity. He grasped her hand, feeling the tears close to the surface as the ceremony was completed. "I love you with all my heart and soul, Emma King, and that will never change as long as I have a breath in me," he murmured as he helped her up.

Emma felt so serene and peaceful as she watched him offer

her what she wanted most in this world. "I love you back, Kenneth King."

They stood and started toward the door, hugging and greeting their parents and friends. Pepper hugged them both so hard, they could barely breathe. "I had a feeling about you two," she said, the tears pooling in her eyes.

"Thank you," Emma said. "For everything."

"I love you both," she said, wiping away her tears and moving down the hall to join the rest of the guests.

Kenneth bent to kiss Emma with all the fervency and intensity of his promise of eternity he had just made. It felt so right. He loved her so much. With all the guests gone before them, they followed the temple worker escorting them down the hall. They stopped in a doorway, near the celestial room and Kenneth pulled out the small wooden jewelry box his grandfather had made for Pepper on their wedding day.

"Pepper gave this to me to give to you on our wedding day. My grandfather gave it to her on her wedding day," he explained. "But I added a little present of my own inside it," he said. "I hope you will be my partner in every way. As my wife and mother to our children and also . . ." He opened the box. "When you get tired of being a city attorney, my partner in law." She took the small card out of the box, and read over the engraved words, "King and King, Attorneys at Law." The look on her face was not what he had expected, and he added hastily. "Only if you want to. Being a mother comes first. You don't even have to leave the house, we could build you an office at home. But I warn you, I need someone like you at my firm and I think we make a good team." He hunched down to look in her eyes. "I'll even let you have all the constitutional law cases."

She laughed and threw her arms around him. "Thank you for not giving up on my dreams."

Kenneth was taken aback. "You're an excellent mother and an excellent lawyer. We're just combining the best of both worlds as long as you want it. Besides, I'm just looking out for my own interests, since I want a good partner I can trust."

Emma wiped away her tears. "I might have to consult my attorney about the particulars, though."

Kenneth folded his arms. "Really? Well, let's see. As a partner, I'm willing to offer you a lifetime of happiness, everything I am and own, and . . . hmm," he smiled a bit wickedly, "twenty-four hour care and personal attention from a very handsome defense lawyer."

Emma was trying to look thoughtful, but he could see right through her. "Has the jury reached a verdict?" he asked

She reached up on her tiptoes and kissed him soundly. "With that kind of offer, how could I refuse?" She took his hand as they walked down the beautifully carved stairs.

Life could not be more perfect, he thought. They belonged together because of the bonds they had forged in adversity. The trials of the past were behind them and while they would remember the lessons learned, now they could look forward to loving each other in the unknown forever in front of them.

ABOUT THE AUTHOR

Julie Coulter Bellon is originally from Lethbridge, Alberta, Canada. She has always been an avid reader and at a young age knew she wanted to be a writer. She graduated from Brigham Young University with a B.A. degree in Secondary Education—English teaching. Julie loves to travel and has been to such places as the Mediterranean and Europe and someday plans to do more. She currently teaches a high school journalism course for Brigham Young University Continuing Education. To indulge her love of books, she also serves on the library board in her community.

Julie and her husband Brian are the parents of six children. She has always enjoyed telling stories and her children like bedtime best when mom tells a "made up" story. When she's not busy being a mom, teaching or writing, you will find her doing family history, playing her flute, preparing her Relief Society lesson or enjoying a family vacation.